Of Prose and Pen

by

Rambling Rose Writers

Createspace

Of Prose and Pen

First published in Great Britain in 2017 by Amazon on Kindle Direct Publishing.

The rights of Rambling Rose Writers to be identified as the Authors of the work in accordance with the Copyright, Designs and Patent Act 1988.

All rights reserved. No part of this publication may be reproduced, stored in a retrieval system, or transmitted, in any form or by any means without the prior written permission of the publisher, nor be otherwise circulated in any form of binding or cover other than that in which it is published and without a similar condition being imposed on the subsequent purchaser.

This book is entirely a work of fiction. The names, characters and incidents portrayed in it are the work of the authors' imaginations. Any resemblance to actual persons, living or dead, events or localities is entirely coincidental.

Sources of Literary quotes:

Chapters one, three, six, seven, ten, eleven & twelve: **www.goodreads.com**

Chapters two and eight: **www.azquotes.com**

Chapters four, five & nine: **www.brainyquotes.com**

All rights reserved. No part of this publication may be reproduced, stored in a retrieval system, or transmitted, in any form or by any means, electronic, mechanical, photocopying, recording or otherwise, without the prior permission of the publishers.

Copyright © Rambling Rose Writers

All Rights Reserved

Of Prose and Pen

AN INTRODUCTION TO RAMBLING ROSE WRITERS

The seeds of our collective literary journey were planted when we started our own writing group. All of us budding authors with a passion for the written word. The initial cultivating of ideas began with thought provoking topics which inspired us to write in our own individual styles. Every week we endeavoured to come up with new ideas or concepts as a base for our poetry, flash fiction, short stories and stories for children. Over the past months, we have been concentrating on pruning and perfecting our work for this publication.

Rambling Rose Writers is developing. Our name stems from our easy (rambling) approach, to propagate our styles and ideas. Our chosen individual pen names, are; Red, Jasmine, Lavender and Cornflower. Our illustrious illustrator is Silver Rose and our guest contributors are Fuchsia and Black.

We hope you enjoy reading our stories.

Each Rose brings a different attribute to the Rambling Rose Writers Group;

<u>Amanda Coulton</u>
Red Rose   *Website Wizard*

<u>Dawn Bligh</u>
Lavender Rose   *Punctuation Pundit*

<u>Pat Ferguson</u>
Jasmine Rose   *Grammar Guru*

<u>Pauline Ludgate</u>
Cornflower Rose   *Document Dynamo*

We welcome your feedback and support.

Please contact us on:

Email: ramblingrosewriters@mail.com

Facebook: Rambling Rose Writers

Twitter: RamblingRoseWriters @RoseWriters

Our chosen charity is Bright Red

"50% of profits from the sale of this book are being donated to Bright Red, a blood cancer charity dedicated to improving the lives and treatment of people in the north of England, who are dealing with blood cancer."

CONTENTS:

Chapter One: Characters   **13**

Miranda's Tail – Cornflower	15
A Story for Sarah – Jasmine	20
Marrti is a Martian – Lavender	24
Polly in L.A. – Red	31

Chapter Two: The Bouquet   **37**

Intrigue – Cornflower	39
A Message from America – Jasmine	44
The Bouquet – Lavender	51
Him Who I Hate – Red	54

Chapter Three: <u>Odd Socks</u>   **57**

Adam's Story – Cornflower   59
Finding Me - Jasmine   64
Amelia's Socks - Lavender   75
Odd Socks - Red   81

Chapter Four: <u>Strangers</u>   **82**

Lenny's House – Cornflower   84
Designs of the Heart – Jasmine   87
The Party – Lavender   99
The Ruined Frangipanes - Red   101

Chapter Five: <u>Was It a Dream?</u>   **103**

The White Feather – Cornflower   105
Jenny's Dream - Jasmine   108
Wings 'n' Things – Lavender   111
Was It Just a Dream? - Red   117

Chapter Six: <u>Who's that?</u>   **122**

Suspicion - Cornflower   124
Man of Mystery – Jasmine   130
Who's that in the Photo? – Lavender   140
Abigail - Red   143

Chapter Seven: <u>Do It now!</u>   **145**

Episodes - Cornflower   147
Tough Love – Jasmine   148
In Training – Lavender   150
Sid – Red   154

Chapter Eight: <u>Lucy Drummond</u>   **157**

The Babysitter – Cornflower   159
Living the Dream – Jasmine   164
Sea-Drum – Lavender   169
Feeling Blue - Red   173

Chapter Nine: <u>Burgundy Boots</u>   **178**

The Little Box - Cornflower   180
A Different Horizon – Jasmine   184
Muck Not Luck - Lavender   191
Gretchen's Gift - Red   195
The Pit – Black   199

Chapter Ten: <u>War</u>   **200**

The Letter – Cornflower   202
Alternative Existence – Jasmine   207
The World Anew – Lavender   209
The Grandmasters' Game - Red   215

Chapter Eleven: <u>Articles</u> **219**

Herbal Remedy - Cornflower 221
Spoken in Confidence – Jasmine 227
Phyllis – Lavender 228
The Sorry Tale of Ted and Tallulah - 232
                                            Red

Chapter Twelve: <u>Poetry</u> **235**

Poetry by Guest Writer Fuchsia Rose 237

Chapter One

"Don't interrupt when your characters take a flight of their own"

Pawan Mishra

Characters

As a way of really getting to know each other at the beginning of our creative process, we used the old and tried method of interviewing each other. This chapter's stories show how, when given free rein, we have created crazy settings and bizarre scenarios, allowing our imaginations to soar.

MIRANDA'S TAIL *by Cornflower Rose*

The spring evening was cool, the light was fading and the moon cast its burnished sheen on the shimmering waves as I walked along the shore. I was hoping the walk and fresh air would relieve the pounding headache that had plagued me all day. I was under a lot of stress at work and I really needed a holiday and some time out to de-stress and clear my mind. So, I wasn't paying much attention to my surroundings.

Strolling along I became aware of a body rising then going down under the water. I watched from the shallow water's edge as the figure rose, then went under again and after what seemed like an age didn't reappear. Panicking, I splashed straight into the waves shouting, "Hang on I'm coming!" thinking whoever it was might be in difficulty. I was soon close enough to put my hand in the water and grab hold of an arm, which I yanked and pulled with all my might and felt the resistant struggle of the person in my grasp.

"Let me go, leave me alone!" cried a little voice.

"No, I won't let you do this to yourself. I'm not going to let you drown," I said through gritted teeth.

"But you don't understand I'm not drowning, please let me go." At that we both fell onto the wet sand.

I wasn't prepared for the sight before my eyes. Half human and half fish. Was it possible? I never thought such things existed, that they were just invented for folklore and Disney films!

She, as she was most definitely female, had the most glorious mane of long, lustrous locks of blonde hair that cascaded down to her waist, preserving her modesty. Her skin was luminous and dark and smooth as silk. Her eyes of cobalt blue pierced me like a steely dagger. I stole a glance at the lower part of her body and knew that she was no myth. From the waist down, she was like a fish with fins and a spreading tail covered in scales.

Speechless, shaking and shivering we sat up on the sand.

She caught me scrutinising her body. "Yes, I'm a Mermaid." She whispered in my ear, "If you give me half a chance I'll tell you my story."

And what a story it was.

"The correct term for me really is a Merrow," she said, "as I am one of those strange beings that although, I have the attributes of a Mermaid, I am more human than fish. I live the majority of my life as a human and only when the calling gets too great, do I seek the sea and become one with it again. The combination of the smell of the salty air and the feel of the salty water on my body is all it takes to transform my legs into a fantail and my lungs transform to allow me to swim deep in the ocean. I try to avoid the sea most of the time but when I can no longer ignore the call, I slip away at night and indulge myself in solitude. I've kept this secret sea-life of mine hidden until now. I have a son, called Finley and I suppose you would call him a Merman, although like me he's more human, like his father, who left us long ago. Fin's way of coping with his life was to join the Navy and live a life on the ocean waves."

Totally stunned, I nodded and listened intently as she continued her story.

"All Mermaids love music and I love playing my ukulele, badly I'm afraid," she said with a wry, self-mocking smile. "But it's a lonely existence and I just long to find a companion who will understand and accept me as I am. But I daren't reveal myself, for fear of being hounded, ridiculed and pointed out as a freak of nature. I'm destined to live solitary for the remainder of my life," she said softly and lowered her head. She had a sad look in her eyes.

I was beginning to become smitten, there was just something wholly innocent and beguiling about her demeanour. I remained silent sensing there was more to her story.

Continuing, she said, "I cope by writing romantic novels where the heroine usually wins the heart of the dashing young man, always with a happy ending. I wish I could write a happy ending for myself where Mr Darcy or Mr Right comes and sweeps me off my feet and we can live happily ever after," she sighed.

I was enchanted by her and curious to know her better, so we agreed to meet a week later in a drier environment.

That chance encounter was a week ago, and now I'm sitting in a Bistro waiting for her to arrive. I felt there was a spark between us and I really liked her regardless of her not being totally human. It didn't bother me once she'd explained everything about her strange lifestyle, I thought it quite a turn on.

Nothing prepared me for the sight that beheld my eyes as she walked into the Bistro. She was beautiful and all eyes were on her as she seemed to glide across the room towards me. It was obvious from the look in her eyes that she liked what she saw too.

"Hello, I'm glad you decided to meet me, I would really like to get to know you better, if you'll let me?"

"I would love to, but maybe we should start off with proper introductions." Holding out her hand she took mine in hers and said, "My name's Miranda Trighton, pleased to meet you."

"Pleased to meet you Miranda I'm Sebastian Wright, how do you do?"

Miranda laughed out loud and said that maybe I was her Mr Right and could be the man of her dreams?

I thought, 'Yes.' I could just be the one to sweep her off her feet or tail whichever one she prefers, it makes no difference to me.

A STORY FOR SARAH by Jasmine Rose

Fran had no idea where her life was going. She knew she had done the right thing when she retired but she had not expected to feel so empty. She had loved her work, it had brought fulfilment and purpose to her life. The change had brought good things of course, it was great to be able to spend more time with her family and her visits to the cottage were much more frequent but, 'there's something missing,' she admitted to herself. She loved the cottage, the familiarity of it. Childhood memories insinuated themselves into every action, the landscape enveloped her - she was part of it, everything fitted. Fran wished she could stay a little longer but she knew it was time to go back.

"Hi Mum," called a voice from the kitchen as she opened the front door. It was her son, James, "Thought I'd provide a welcoming committee for you," he said as he gave her a hug. "Can't stay long, I just wanted to hear about Scotland, I so wish I could have been there with you."

They ate a late, leisurely lunch together then, as he was leaving, he remembered to tell her that her friend Margo had rung while she was away.

"Something about a project she is involved in, she wants you to call her back."

"I haven't spoken to Margo in ages," Fran said as she waved him goodbye. "I wonder what she is up to now?"

As soon as he left Fran rang her friend.

"Oh Fran, it is so good to hear your voice." But Margo's tone belied the usual good spirits which Fran normally associated with her friend, there was a kind of wearied ebullience about it. They chatted for a few minutes then Margo gave Fran a broad outline of the work she was involved in, helping refugees and asylum seekers.

"We're up to our eyes with preparing applications, meeting housing needs – all the practical stuff, but they need more Fran. There are so many stories to tell and I think you would be able to help them."

"I'm not so sure about that," Fran responded, "wouldn't language be a problem?"

"I don't think so," Margo replied quickly, "we have an interpreter and what we would want you to do is help to record not only the facts but the emotions which underpin them. You make wonderful use of language Fran and these stories need to be told. We want the human touch. I want you to meet Saida, one of our interpreters. Come tomorrow, stay overnight and we will go to the Centre on Wednesday."

"Ok but I am making no promises," said Fran cautiously. She remembered how persuasive Margo could be!

When she got off the train she could see her friend waving frantically beyond the ticket barrier. Seeing her beaming face lifted Fran's spirits. 'My goodness how I've missed her,' she thought and berated herself for letting the friendship slip over the past couple of years. They hugged each other.

"Right," Margo said, "today is for us – tomorrow it is down to business!"

Next day they arrived at the Refugee Centre quite early. Fran felt quite overwhelmed by the intensity of suppressed emotions surrounding her. She could sense fear, anxiety, anger, resignation and relief, but no hope. The thought saddened her. Margo took her to meet Saida and she knew immediately that they would get along. Saida walked with soothing calmness through the negativity and despondency which threatened to envelope everyone around her.

"Come with me Fran, I want you to meet Sarah. She arrived a few days ago." Saida took her to Sarah's room. As they entered, the young woman standing next to the window turned to meet them and her eyes rested on Fran - black, beguiling, bruised. Sarah had had to fight to survive the journey from her homeland. She was holding her new-born. She had fought for two.

Fran approached slowly and touched Sarah's hand, her gaze resting on the baby. Sarah loosened his blanket and allowed her to look at her son. His eyes were fixed on Sarah's face, they were black, beguiling and beautiful. His solid, rounded little body snuggled against his mother, an armful of plumpiousness. Sarah cooed gently as she turned her face to him. Fran sensed that this baby was the only joy in Sarah's life and she wanted more for her. Saida introduced them to each other and Fran felt a burgeoning resolve rising within her. Sarah's story would be told.

MARRTI *by Lavender Rose*

"Marrti is a Martian,"

"Marrti is a Martian,"

Sue has been listening to re-runs of Top of the Pops and as she was singing the words in her head to the tune of Jilted John's, 'Gordon is a Moron,' she realised the truth in her words. Even her name made it obvious!

Marrti had been her neighbour since they were eleven. Both had been brought up by their mothers and both had found their own homes in the same area. Marrti had been her co-conspirator, her comforter and her companion. Her bubbly, brightly dressed buddy. Enigmatic, excitable, exquisite. Yet a maddening man magnet. Sue had attributed it to her long legs, long blond hair and luscious cleavage, but now the evidence pointed in an entirely different direction…

Marrti often delegated little jobs she could easily have done herself if she'd remembered. As Sue worked in an office about 5 minutes from their homes and Marrti worked about a 20-minute drive away, today Sue had been commanded to use her key to pop into her friend's house and collect an urgent letter to post. But her morning coffees had caught her out, she needed the loo, fast. As she ventured upstairs she noticed the open loft ladder. Time was pressing, but curiosity was pressing harder, so after a speedy loo visit she climbed, only intending a quick peek. She'd never been in her friend's attic before and wondered if it was as tidy and minimal as the rest of the house?

In sci-fi films alien crafts are often depicted as floating orbs. Here was exactly that! "Rrrrrrrrrrrrrrrrr," it droned, reminding her of the extra r's Marrrrrrrti added when she signed her name! (name signed electronically). On the walls were some posters of The Red Planet. On a low table were dozens of cartons holding see-through, 'jumping-bean' like clear vials. Inside each one was what looked like a moving hologram of a person. All men.

On closer inspection Sue realised she recognised some of the guys. Fourth along was unmistakably Dave, Marrti's first boyfriend. Frozen in time, looking exactly as he'd looked at sixteen. Athletic, handsome, clever. After they'd broken up he'd seemed to give up and never made much of his life. A few other strangers, then there was a past window cleaner, the guy who previously owned the corner shop, their old dentist (who had suddenly lost his nerve and his job). She noticed several more in the long chain of boyfriends Marrti had strung along over the years. Inside the vials they looked immortalised in their past prime. But most were now jobless and living in poverty, yet faithful followers in Marrti's male harem.

There was their friends husband Evan, who'd been a keen designer and studied architecture at university. She'd thought the pressure had got too much and that's why he'd dropped out. He was now a hollow shell who'd split with his wife and now walked in Marrti's shadow. A loyal follower, willing to accept scraps of affection along with lurid email communications. Sue had hastily stopped viewing those linked emails! Come to think of it Dave and the long list of exes and many other guys she saw here had been on that communication list as well.

One Christmas there'd been a talented, but smelly busker outside their local. Marrti had invited him inside. She'd ignored our group and plied him with drink and had talked to him for ages, then horror of horrors Sue had noticed her kiss him as he was leaving. Here was his likeness preserved.

Person after person, all suspended in time. Many she recognised, including celebrities. In common they all now shared damaged, weakened lives. Costly kisses causing chaos? What had been stolen and was being kept here? Their essence? Their vitality? Was that why their lives had changed so radically?

Sue had to go. She posted the letter and she took the rest of the day off work. She needed to walk as it helped her to think.

She reflected on when she first met her partner and the dread of introducing him to Marrti in case he fell under her seeming spell. Fortunately, he'd never particularly liked Marrti (which had proved awkward on many occasions). Similarly, as Sue's son was growing older she was terrified that he would become interested in Marrti. Thankfully so far he'd been immune, unlike other youngsters who flocked round their neighbourhood, time-wasters who were more than happy to do anything for Marrti.

Why had some succumbed, but others resisted her fatal charm? As she puzzled over this conundrum she saw Dave and Evan in her mind's eye, both saying, "Mines a pint." She could remember every captee she knew well saying the exact same thing. But her husband drank wine. Her son was in his mid-teens and oddly refused to touch alcohol. She thought of other men who were joint acquaintances and drank wine. None of them had been in the loft crew.

There had only been two empty vials left at end of the tray. Was time running out? Could she rescue the trapped guys? Would their essences be taken back to Mars or could they find the way back to their human bodies? How could she help?

The vials had all been sealed. If she dropped one on the floor would the person trapped inside be injured? She couldn't risk it! These guys had already lost enough of their lives.

What about the wine and tee total thing? Were they all beer drinkers? Could it really be as simple as that?

She could have a party for all the fellas she knew and try insisting they drink wine, but she didn't recognise loads of the men there, so chances of finding them all would be zero.

Maybe… She knew Marrti would be home at four. She had some money and might just have time. She dashed to the corner shop and bought a bottle of cheap fizzy wine. She returned to Marrti's and let herself in.

Just as Sue was nearing the landing at the top of the stairs she heard heels tapping down the path outside. Maybe this was a bad idea! Perhaps she should have waited till another day. But the chances of the loft being open again were almost none existent, this might be the only opportunity she would get.

She heard the key in the door as she quickly scrambled up the loft ladder.
She heard the front door open and close as she fumbled in her bag.
She heard the heels on the stairs as she took out the bottle. "Who's there?" demanded Marrti, as Sue frantically shook the bottle. Fumbling with the wire over the cork Sue tried to act naturally as she watched Marrti's head appear.
The cork exploded with a magnificent 'pop,' and mock champagne whooshed out covering everything in the loft. The vials seemed to evaporate and each hologram floated down from the loft. Hopefully they'd return to their rightful owners. Marrti was evaporating and hissing, "My worrrrk, spoiled!"

A cold type of breeze passed Sue. An opening appeared in the pod and then disappeared. Everything felt cold and with a reducing, "rrrrrrrrrrr," then a silent shimmer the pod disappeared.

Sue felt shaken. She wasn't sure exactly what had happened.

Even as she was walking distractedly down the stairs a lady called Marrti was walking into the apartment above a busy bistro in Paris. "Bonjour monsieur," she said, smiling enticingly at a passing neighbour…

POLLY IN L.A. *by Red Rose*

Polly was a wife, mother and grandmother. She also held down the demanding role of Admin Manager in a male orientated office. It wasn't easy but she enjoyed it, and what a proud moment when she was nominated for the title of Charity Champion. She had raised thousands of pounds for the local hospice over the years and it was lovely to be appreciated. Because of all her good work an anonymous benefactor had donated £10,000 and gifted her and a work colleague an all-expenses paid trip to Los Angeles for seven days.

So, after much planning and holiday shopping, she finally arrived on Hollywood Boulevard and found herself checking into the Hotel Roosevelt. She looked around her room in awe taking in every little detail, it oozed extravagance. Throwing herself down onto the huge king size bed, she sank into the luxuriously soft mattress and felt like royalty. It was another world. This was how the other half lived.

The next day off she went, on her own, to the Hollywood Boulevard Walk of Fame and came across a Hollywood Stars photo booth. It superimposed a photo of yourself next to the star of your choice. Of course Polly had to have one taken with Mel Gibson. Oh those eyes... she'd fallen in love with him many years ago after watching him play Fletcher Christian in The Bounty.

As she sat there in her best pose, a leather clad hand rudely pushed through the curtains throwing a black briefcase onto the floor. Polly cursed as the flash went off, and the photo was taken. The prints arrived displaying an unflattering picture of her shocked face, her mouth agape. Heart pounding, she peered out through the curtains, people were going about their business as normal, nothing seemed untoward. Gingerly she picked up the briefcase and decided to make her way back to the safety of her hotel room so she could think clearly about her next move.

Her head in a whirl she placed the unopened briefcase carefully on to the bed, then started to question her actions. What the heck was she doing... it could contain a bomb, she jumped as the sound of ringing came from inside. "Here goes," she grimaced, turning away, as she clicked it open. There was a mobile phone inside with, 'Unknown Caller' flashing up on the screen.

Quietly cautious she answered, "Hello."

A voice replied, "Listen to me carefully, there is a blue folder in the briefcase, inside it you will find a padded envelope addressed to Scott Garcia. Please ring the phone number written on the front, arrange to meet him and hand it over in person. Tell him it's from Larry. It is imperative you do not give it to anyone else." His tone had a sense of urgency, she started to speak but he cut her short. "My life depends upon it, time is of the essence, I beg you do not contact the police," then he hung up.

She stared at the phone, poured a glass of wine then picked up said envelope, she felt like she was in a Bruce Willis movie; things like this didn't happen to her!

Larry Bloom skulked unobtrusively away from the pay phone, hoping and praying he could trust this woman to do as he asked. He was a journalist for the Daily Breeze and had received an anonymous tip off about two bent cops working for the Los Angeles Police Department. He had footage of them taking money from a local drug dealer, but when he tried to report it the proverbial had hit the fan, and now someone had planted 'Class A' drugs in his apartment. They were trying to frame him. Luckily he escaped out of the fire exit and was now living rough in a cardboard box on Skid Row, in the hope this mess would be cleared up and that truth would prevail. This story would either make his career or kill him! After he had thrown the briefcase into the photo booth he lurked in the background following Polly back to her hotel before he made contact.

Polly took another swig of wine then examined the envelope, it was sealed but she could feel the shape of a CD inside it. Taking a deep breath, she dialled the phone number that was handwritten on the front. It rang and a male voice answered, "Yes?"

Polly stuttered, "Can I speak to Scott Garcia please?"

"Speaking, who is this?"

"My name is Polly, all I know is I have an envelope for you from Larry Bloom."

His voice was hushed, "Right, let me think, I've got a show tonight but I can meet you before, let's say 7.30, the corner of Melrose Avenue," and he hung up. She sighed, putting her head in her hands. What was she getting herself into?

Polly prided herself on being punctual so she arrived at the meeting place ten minutes early. Unbeknown to her Larry Bloom had followed and was watching from across the street, to make sure the envelope was delivered. An old red Mustang pulled up and a drag queen jumped out, wearing the most fabulous leopard print dress and the highest shoes Polly had ever seen.

"You have something for me?"

Polly was taken aback, "Erm yes, what's your name?"

"I'm Scott Garcia, female impersonator to the stars sweet cheeks, quick give me the envelope."

As the sound of sirens rang out in the distance Larry ran across the road towards them. "Get in the car," he shouted as shots rang out. Scott screamed as a bullet scraped his ankle and he went over on his stilettos. "I can't drive," he shrieked.

Larry bundled him into the back of the Mustang then leapt into the passenger seat shouting, "Go, go!" then started to wheeze as Polly jumped into the driver's side and took off at breakneck speed, adrenaline kicking in, taking the corners almost on two wheels whilst trying to ignore the criticism coming from Scott. One of her pet hates was back seat drivers.

With alarm, she took a sidelong look at Larry Bloom in the passenger seat, as his face turned first grey then purple. He grappled in his pockets, finally managing to fish out his inhaler, which after one big heave, eased his gasps. Trying to stay calm she kept glancing in the mirror at Scott as he alternated between barking out directions and sobbing with anguish about his injury.

After what seemed like an age they eventually screeched to a halt outside an impressive house with electric gates that opened as they approached. Polly turned to Larry and Scott whose faces were ashen, "They don't call me Super Gran for nothing you know," she said. Larry muttered something under his breath as they clambered out of the Mustang.

An imposing man in a black suit was waiting in the doorway to take them inside. He was the LAPD Police Commander and Scott Garcia's father. The envelope containing the incriminating evidence was handed over. Scott was ferried to hospital, arrests were made and justice was done.

Larry Bloom went back to his job at the Daily Breeze with a promotion in the offing. Scott Garcia had to cancel his drag queen shows for a few weeks until the swelling went down on his ankle, and he could squeeze back into his stilettos.

Polly stayed long-dis buddies with them both and oh, what a story she had to tell her grandchildren when she got home.

Chapter Two

"Of all flowers, me thinks a Rose is best"

William Shakespeare

- The Two Noble Kinsmen

The Bouquet

'I noticed the beautiful flower arrangement and wondered who could possibly have sent them…'

It's amazing how a comment about a beautiful flower arrangement can result in such different stories.

INTRIGUE *by Cornflower Rose*

I noticed the beautiful flower arrangement and wondered who could possibly have sent it?

Sitting resplendent on Mary's desk, they looked strangely at odds with the plethora of books, files and papers littering her disordered work space. Known as the office workaholic; dowdy, unfashionably dressed, middle-aged Mary always preferred her own company. No-one could recall her ever attending social evenings or special lunches or hospitality provided by the company. Any attempt from a sympathetic colleague was always met by a glassy-eyed stare and a quick rebuff. She was an enigma to all her co-workers. Needless to say, people tended to leave her to her own devices.

But the arrival of the flowers aroused an awful lot of curiosity. Unfortunately, I was nominated with the task of trying to establish who the sender may be.

My first attempt…

"Hi Mary, lovely flowers, have you got a secret admirer?"

"Well, Malcolm, that's for me to know and you to find out!" she snapped, as she dismissed me, turning away.

Later, my second attempt…

"Can I get you a tea or coffee Mary?" whilst trying to sneak a look to see if there was a gift card attached.

"No thanks Malcolm I don't like tea and coffee gives me a migraine," she sniffed haughtily.

Much later, my third attempt…

"Can I borrow your pencil sharpener please Mary? I seem to have misplaced mine."

"Malcolm, I think you need to have your eyes tested because I can quite clearly see it on your desk from here!" she replied, giving me the death stare.

This was becoming more of a challenge than I anticipated.

Signalling covertly to my fellow colleagues Sally, Bernard and Jacinta, I pointed to the kitchen. We needed to regroup and form another plan. I decided we should find another tactic if we were to ever shed light on the mystery admirer.

"Look guys, it's near impossible to engage Mary in a meaningful conversation of any kind, we are going to have to be a lot smarter about it," I wheedled.

"Well!" said Sally, "What about if I were to distract her for a minute and Malcolm you can sneak past and look for a card. It's obvious she won't tell us if we ask her."

"If she wasn't such a workaholic staying behind until everyone's gone home on a night, we could easily find out. She never leaves her desk long enough to get near," bemoaned Bernard.

"Right, it's settled then," said Sally, "I'll think of some distraction and you Malcolm be ready to pounce – OK?"

On tenterhooks and trying to concentrate on my tasks at hand I was constantly on the look-out for a sign from Sally that she was going to do the deed. Working silently I was slightly distracted by a work problem, so my blood froze on hearing a piercing scream.

I jumped up and quickly strode to the side of Mary's desk.

"Arrggghhh!" screamed Sally again, "Look Mary there's a mouse just ran under your desk." Mary sprang into action, and dropped under her desk with her shoe in her hand.

"Where are you? You little beggar!" screeched Mary.

I leaned over her desk to peer at the flowers but inadvertently knocked a pile of books, which had been precariously stacked on the edge of the desk. On toppling over, they'd pushed the vase of flowers and it fell to the floor. I dropped to my knees just as Mary came out from under her desk and the pair of us banged heads with a resounding crack! The flowers lay squashed and scattered on the ground amongst a pile of soggy books under the chipped vase. My heart was racing as I sat up and saw Mary looking stunned on the floor beside me.

"What the hell do you think you are playing at you fool?" she cried. "Look at my flowers – oh and my books!"

Running around the desk I tried to scoop up the contents of the vase and brushed off the books. There, under the flowers, was the object of my investigation - a card. I picked it up sharply and stuffed it in my pocket. I tidied up the mess as best I could and arranged the flowers to the best of my ability. Meanwhile Sally was explaining to Mary that she must have been seeing things as it was obvious there was no mouse about.

I escaped as soon as I could into the kitchen to look at the card I'd toiled so hard to find.

Hand written in a neat italic script the card, from an expensive flower emporium, read:

Mary,

Thank you for all your hard work and commitment in helping to make this company a success.

I really appreciate everything you do (and I mean <u>everything!</u>)

See you tonight for another special evening together.
Love always,
Jim B xxx

Jim B? Jim B? Surely there could only be one Jim B? Crikey! Could it be that Mary is the secret love interest of our illustrious CEO? Why the sly old dog Mary, it just goes to show you shouldn't judge a book by its cover!

Well one thing's for sure the others aren't going to believe this and I couldn't wait to enlighten them.

A MESSAGE FROM AMERICA *by Jasmine Rose*

Jane really enjoyed her visits to Nightingale Nursing Home, she'd definitely done the right thing volunteering to work there each week. It was warm and welcoming and she felt the residents there were well cared for. Most of them had regular visitors, which gave Jane more opportunities to spend time with those who didn't. She knew she shouldn't have favourites so she tried to divide her time evenly, but she did have a special affection for Mrs Vickers in room 23.

There was something about Mrs Vickers which made Jane want to try harder to connect with her. The old lady, whose name was Elsa, was almost ninety and very frail. Severe dementia had robbed her of any means of communication. She was unable to speak and had very little mobility, completely dependent on the people who cared for her. Jane tried to piece together the snippets of information she had gleaned from staff and other residents, asking them what they knew about her.

It seemed that Elsa and her husband John had moved into the home about ten years earlier. They were both very musical and Elsa had loved to sing. It was generally believed that she had sung professionally when she was young.
"She had a beautiful voice," those who knew her said. "When they first moved here they used to have weekly concerts in the lounge. People came from outside to hear her perform - it was lovely." "They were such a wonderful couple, absolutely devoted to each other." Sadly, after John had died Elsa's dementia had advanced quite rapidly.

Jane was delighted to learn that Elsa had loved to sing, she loved singing herself - in fact she'd recently joined a choir and eagerly looked forward to each practice. It was great now that the children were growing up and she had more time to pursue her own interests. Matthew was so supportive.

"Go for it love, it's time for you now," he had said to her.

She was so lucky to have Matthew, they had made a good life together.
Goodness me, seventeen years married and he's

still the best thing that has happened to me, she mused.

As far as Jane knew, no-one else visited Elsa. It seemed she had no children. There was no-one close to her plus she wasn't an easy person to visit being so difficult to engage with. Visitors gave up, thinking that she was not even aware of them in the room. Jane remembered being told that hearing was often the last of the senses to go and she believed that it was possible for Elsa to hear her even though she couldn't respond. She made up her mind to make her visits as rich as possible for the old lady.

Each week she talked about herself, her family and whatever was happening in the world - anything and everything, and as she talked she held Elsa's hand. During one visit Jane told Elsa about the choir and about how much she loved singing again. They were rehearsing the song 'Memories' from the musical Cats and Jane started to softly sing it, keeping her eyes on Elsa's face. She could hardly believe it when she felt a slight pressure from the frail fingers which had rested lifelessly in her hand. She knew Elsa was listening! At last a connection had been made and Jane's visits became a mix of talking and singing.

When Jane entered Elsa's room one day, the first thing she noticed was a beautiful bouquet of flowers. She wondered who could possibly have sent them? As far as she knew she had been the only visitor for some time. Sally, one of the care assistants, followed Jane into the room.

"Hi Jane," she said, "The flowers came at lunchtime, special delivery. Aren't they gorgeous! Our manager, Mrs Carlysle, would like to see you before you talk to Elsa, is that ok?"

"Yes of course, I'll go now." Jane went straight to the manager's office.

"Jane, I'm so glad you've come today. Come in and sit down."

When Jane was seated Mrs Carlysle told her of a telephone call she had taken the previous day. It was from an American lady explaining that she was sending the flowers on behalf of her grandfather who had died recently. He had known Elsa during the war years when he was stationed in the North of England.

She understood Elsa was a singer and they met when the band she worked with had been hired to come to their base to entertain the troops. Her Grandpa was obviously very fond of her and she'd recently helped him to find out if Elsa was still living. They managed to trace her to our nursing home.

She had also explained to Mrs Carlysle that she was unable to visit because her stay in England was short but she had forwarded a letter to be delivered with the flowers. It was addressed to Elsa, written by her grandfather. She had found it among his personal papers after his death, with a request to forward it to Elsa.

Mrs Carlysle handed the letter to Jane.

"Elsa can't read it but we know that she responds to you, she recognises your voice. Will you read it to her Jane please? I know you are fond of her and I can't think of anyone better to ask."

Jane returned to Elsa's room and sat next to her. She looked at the empty face as she opened the letter.

"Hello Elsa, I have a surprise message today, meant especially for you!" She took hold of the frail hand waiting patiently on the bed cover and read,

To my lovely Elsa,

I hope you will one day read this letter because I want you to know that, even though we both knew our time together couldn't last, you have occupied a place in my heart since the day we first met. The war years were a time like no

other. A time set apart, during which you and I were blessed to enter each other's lives. I fell in love with you the first time you came to entertain us at the base where we were stationed. How vibrant and beautiful you were, with the voice of an angel.

I hope the years since have been good for you Elsa and you found happiness with someone deserving of your love, someone who shared your intensity and passion for music. You were right, even though I didn't want to believe you at the time; my home is here with my wife and children. I have spoken of you many times and, miraculously, my granddaughter has been able to find you, using the Internet in ways I will never understand!

Thank you, Elsa for the joy and passion we shared. My life was altered through knowing you and I hope I have been a better man because of you. I send my love and gratitude for the memories which have never left me.

*Your friend forever,
Michael.*

Jane folded the letter and placed it in Elsa's hand. She saw the bony fingers close round it and she gently stroked Elsa's arm.

"Do you remember this Elsa?" She started to sing the first song that came into her head.

"We'll meet again, don't know where..." Tears came into her eyes as she saw Elsa's face softening and she caught her breath as she witnessed the frozen lips move ever so slightly. Jane bent forward, her ear close to Elsa's face - a faint sound. Elsa was singing!

THE BOUQUET *by Lavender Rose (suitable to be read with younger children)*

Nan noticed the beautiful flower arrangement and wondered who could possibly have sent it. "Where are the flowers from?" she asked, "Has your mum got an admirer?"
"Nah," laughed Josh. "We did it!"
"Wow! When did you do that?" asked Nan.

He held up his little finger.
"On Monday we went in the garden and at the back we noticed the daffodil buds, so we picked one with a long stalk. We put it in the vase with water, but, the vase wasn't quite full or ready yet."

He held up his little finger and his ring finger. "On Tuesday we went in the garden and on the right we noticed the tulip buds, so we picked two with long stalks. We added them to the vase but the vase wasn't quite full or ready yet."

He held up his little finger, his ring finger and his middle finger.
"On Wednesday we went in the garden and at the

front we noticed the poppy buds, so we picked three with long stalks. We added them to the vase but the vase wasn't quite full or ready yet."

He held up his little finger, his ring finger, his middle finger and his pointing finger.
"On Thursday we went in the garden and on the left we noticed the bluebells in bud, so we picked four with long stalks. We added them to the vase but the vase wasn't quite full or ready yet."

He held up his little finger, his ring finger, his middle finger, his pointing finger and his thumb.
"On Friday we went in the garden and in the centre we noticed the rose buds, so we picked five with long stalks. We added them to the vase with water but the vase wasn't full or quite ready yet."

He held up his little finger, his ring finger, his middle finger, his pointing finger, his thumb and his other little finger.
"On Saturday we came in the front room and we looked at the vase. All the flower buds were beginning to open, the vase was nearly full but the vase wasn't quite full or ready yet."

He held up his little finger, his ring finger, his middle finger, his pointing finger, his thumb, his other little finger and his other ring finger.
"On Sunday, this morning, Mum showed me what she'd found under her bed. It was this

beautiful green ribbon and she helped me tie it in a bow around the vase. The flowers were in full bloom, and the vase was full and ready."

"They look amazing," said Nan.

"Happy Birthday," said Josh and Mum. "We picked our flowers as a present to put in the vase we bought for you."

"We made a cake as well," said Josh.

"Let's eat it in the garden," suggested Mum, "its lovely outside and our spring flowers are just beginning to bloom."

"I can help you blow out all your candles," said Josh.

To think about...
What colour flowers had Josh and Mum picked for Nan?
Are those flowers always the same colours as in the story?
How many days did it take to fill the vase?
How many flowers were in the vase?
Where do you see flowers?
Why should you wash your hands after picking flowers?
What does the Country Code say about picking flowers?
What's your favourite flower?

'HIM WHO I HATE' *by Red Rose*

As I made myself comfortable in my usual chair, I noticed the beautiful flower arrangement and wondered who could possibly have sent them. I lived five doors down, but often paid her a visit and she was always pleased to see me.

She talked her usual nonsensical chatter as she went about her business, "Where were you yesterday Charlie? I missed you." I gazed at her languidly through half closed eyes. Doesn't she realise I have a life to lead, places to go, people to see.

My dozing was rudely interrupted as the front door burst open and I leapt up with a start. Peace had ended, it was 'Him who I Hate.'

"Stay there Charlie, it's only Roger," her voice soothed as she walked over to greet him.

"Thank you for the flowers darling, what a lovely surprise."

I didn't like him and the feeling was mutual. He had allergies and said I made him uncomfortable. He tolerated me when she was around but whenever she left the room he would lock eyes with me and glare. But I was the victor, I always managed to stare him out.

He ignored me as they embraced, then he started to sneeze. "Oh Roger, come into the kitchen," she said, fussing over him like an anxious mother hen.

While they were out of the room I took the chance to stealthily creep up on the flowers, wanting to have a closer look at what 'Him who I Hate' had sent her. A squint of my eyes, a thrash of my tail and *clatter*! The vase was over, water everywhere and the contents strewn across the floor.

She ran in shrieking as red faced Roger was advancing on me. "That ruddy cat, I'll kill it." With lightning speed, hissing and spitting I made my escape, generously leaving traces of my fur in the air for him to inhale. I jumped up onto the safe sanctuary of the garden fence with all my nine lives still intact.

Feeling smugly satisfied, I peered through the patio door observing the chaotic scene inside. 'Him who I Hate' had started to sneeze again.

"Oh I do hope he has ran out of antihistamines," I purred, turning my back on them as I jumped down off the fence, sprayed against the shed and carried on with my travels.

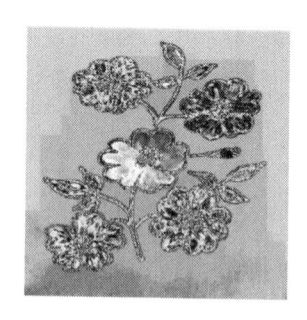

Chapter Three

"One can never have enough socks" said Dumbledore. "Another Christmas has gone and I didn't get a single pair. People will insist on giving me books"

J.K. Rowling

~ Harry Potter and the Sorcerer's Stone

Odd Socks

'Amelia looked down at her feet, smiled and wriggled her toes, she liked to wear odd socks…'

We've all done it by accident, but it's more interesting to explore why they might be worn this way on purpose. Some reasons are sinister, some bittersweet and others just plain mischievous.

ADAM'S STORY *by Cornflower Rose*

Amelia looked down at her feet, smiled and wriggled her toes, she liked to wear odd socks. Wearing them like that evoked so many bittersweet memories. Poignantly she smiled as thoughts of Adam sprang to mind. Dear, sweet, lovely Adam. She will always love him until the day she dies. How could she not? He had been her saviour. As usual her meandering thoughts turned from sweet to bitter, as memories from her early life came flooding back and made her feel emotional.

In her mind's eye was a picture of herself at six years old, blonde curly hair, blue eyes, red from crying, standing on the doorstep of what was to be her new home. She would never forget feeling frightened, lonely and miserable as she was handed over to her new foster parents, who welcomed her with smiling faces and friendly words. Oh! How clever they had been to conceal their true natures, as they turned out to be mean, nasty, spiteful individuals. She was soon to learn just how horrible they were, first hand, when they singled her out for 'special treatment.' She had been the youngest of the four foster children, so was the easier target for their anger and spite. Being new to the home, she didn't have the nerve to stand up for herself, so, keeping her head down, tried to be as pliable as possible. This meant she was put on even more. Made to wash the dishes, clean up after the slovenly pair and see to it that the beds were made and sheets washed for everyone. The other foster kids were just as miserable as they too had chores of their own, so left her to it. Except Adam of course. He was ten, and had taken pity on her. Whenever possible he deflected some of the mistreatment from the adults and even took beatings for her. They became very close, and she began to seek him out and crave his attention when possible. He was like a real big brother to her, her only true family. They made a little code of their own, something that would only mean something special to them. If she was feeling particularly low, lonely or upset, she would put different coloured socks on. He would know to instantly come to her side and he too would wear odd socks. The foster parents wouldn't allow the children to bond or get close to one another, they liked to keep them apart as much as possible, as any grouping together could mean standing up for themselves. They stamped this out at all times.

All the kids were miserable, underfed and craving attention, but were discouraged from helping each other, so it was important that they kept their secret and would leave little notes for each other whenever possible.

On the face of it, the foster parents were respected and well thought of by the Social Services, and were very clever at concealing the truth of what went on. It was obvious they were only in it for the money. They scrimped on everything. Clothes were recycled, food was poor quality and luxuries were unheard of. Christmas times were dire and no one looked forward to them, but still she didn't care about any of that as long as her and Adam had each other.

Amelia had been there for four years when Adam suddenly became very ill. He had to go to hospital, and no one would tell her anything about him or let her go to visit him. She was distraught and asked for him every day, only to be told to shut up and mind her own business! She cried herself to sleep every night for two weeks, until he returned. It was obvious that he was gravely ill, and he told her he had something called Leukaemia and that they had sent him home as they couldn't do anything more for him. It was only then that they were allowed to spend all their time together, as the foster parents expected her to look after him. She didn't mind, but it was hard as she could see he was fading. She made sure that their time together was special. Every day she ran home from school to Adam, until the day she got home and found he wasn't there. Frantic she searched everywhere crying out for him. They told her he was gone and wouldn't be coming back, and she just had to get over it. They buried Adam a week later when she was at school.

Heartbroken and distraught Amelia barely managed to get through each day, grieving and empty and feeling like she wanted to join him. Then one day another little boy turned up at the foster home. He was about six years old, and looked terrified. His name was David and he cried himself to sleep every night for a week. Amelia started to feel sorry for him as she remembered how she felt when she arrived; lonely, frightened and without a friend in the world. Showing some compassion, she went to him in the night and comforted him. His little face beamed up at her, pleased to see a friendly face. She decided there and then that they should have a little secret of their own, so told him about Adam and their secret odd sock wearing code. He cheered up instantly and was happy to have someone to cling to. It filled Amelia's heart with pleasure as she was sure that Adam would be looking down on her and would be so proud of her carrying on his good deeds to others less fortunate than herself.

Now an adult she thought back to how such an innocent idea could turn out to be something so wonderful. As the Administrator of 'Odd Socks for Adam,' the charity she'd set up, she made sure that one day of the year was dedicated to Adams memory. Everyone was encouraged to wear odd socks. The money raised went to help children in care, like her, Adam and David, to make sure that no-one was left to feel lonely and sad. Special counsellors were funded by the charity and Amelia was proud to say that she was one of them.

FINDING ME *by Jasmine Rose*

Amelia sighed as she approached the building, "What is the matter with me, why do I feel such a loser?"

"The trouble with you," her friend Debbie had said, "is that you let people take advantage of you. You try to please all of the people all of the time; you think everyone is cleverer than you and, it seems to me that you have stopped believing in yourself. It's certainly time you gave Robert short shrift – he treats you like a doormat!" The words had stung, but Debbie was her best friend and wouldn't have said them if she didn't think they were true. Amelia knew she needed to have more faith in herself again and it was up to her to do something about it. That was why she had enrolled for the 'Finding Me' workshops at her local Arts Centre. That was why she was now dragging her leaden feet up the steps to the main entrance!

Panic must have been written large on her face as she walked through the doors because, before she had time to walk straight out, a cheery faced young woman approached her.

"Hi, I'm Susan, have you come for the 'Finding Me' workshops?"

"Yes, but right now I'm regretting it," Amelia replied. "I'm not sure I have done the right thing."

"Most people feel like that at the beginning." Susan smiled, "That's why I am here to meet you. You will never be sure if you don't take the chance."

True to form, Amelia didn't think she had much choice and she passively allowed herself to be guided to the room where the workshops would take place. She heaved a sigh of relief as she scanned the faces of the other occupants, each one looking as apprehensive as herself. She didn't recognise anyone - THANK GOODNESS!

They sat in the obligatory circle and were led through the housekeeping rules and introductory stages of the course contents by a rather attractive man whose name was Ben. He had a lovely voice, Amelia thought - velvety with a hint of tweed. Ben was to be the group facilitator. He had a relaxed, disarming manner about him and, in a short space of time, the group members were able talk a little about themselves and their reasons for being there, without feeling too embarrassed.

Amelia couldn't help but feel attracted to Ben, he was good looking in a craggy kind of way. He gave the impression that he was completely comfortable in his own skin. Her attention was drawn more and more frequently towards him because she couldn't help but notice that he was wearing odd socks! Poor man, she thought, he is going to feel so stupid when he goes home! She refrained from saying anything because she didn't want to embarrass him in front of the group, she didn't know him well enough to be so personal. It seemed to be no time at all before the workshop came to an end and Amelia was pleasantly surprised to discover that she had enjoyed herself. She even found herself agreeing to come back the following week.

"Next week I want you to think of a situation which causes you to behave in a way which leaves you feeling disappointed in yourself. We'll help each other to find a way to address the problem, one which leaves you feeling positive rather than disappointed." When she heard Ben say this Amelia wondered if this would be a good opportunity to make her relationship with her line manager a more equal one.

Amelia loved her job as a Community Development Worker, it was really rewarding to see other people getting the opportunity to work on projects which helped them to determine their own futures. Her main problem was Chloe, her line manager. Chloe always seemed to find a way of taking the credit for Amelia's ideas to promote the educational programme of the organisation they worked for.

"She succeeds because you allow her to," Debbie had said the last time Amelia had been having a moan. She was determined not to let it happen again and she decided to share the problem at the next workshop. She was currently working on an exciting new plan for a horticultural project which could be used to expand the education programme even further. It was a subject really close to her heart and she wanted to present the ideas to their Board of Directors at the next meeting. Chloe usually insisted on doing the presentations herself.

Tuesday evening soon came and Amelia surprised herself by being early. They sat down and Ben took his seat among them, casually crossing his feet. Amelia's eyes nearly popped out of her head! Odd socks! Again!! What was going on with this man? She managed to keep her mouth firmly shut and, as a group, they worked at helping each other to find their capable, more confident selves – the people they used to know but had gradually lost touch with. Amelia walked home that evening with her head held high.

Next morning she arrived early to work and waited for Chloe to come into the office.

"Hi Chloe, I am sorry to swoop so early but I know how busy you are, and I would like to book some supervision time soon."

"Goodness, this sounds urgent," said Chloe as she reached for her diary. "Will 10 o'clock tomorrow do?"

"10 o'clock will be great, thanks Chloe," Amelia responded, suppressing a smile as she saw the look of uncertainty flutter across her manager's face.

The butterflies in her stomach were overly active however as she joined Chloe in the small meeting room the following day. She took heart from the support and encouragement of her Tuesday compatriots - she knew they were rooting for her.

"Well, what is so important Amelia?" Chloe asked after they had exchanged pleasantries.

"I'm working on a new idea to extend the education programme," Amelia replied. "It is based on the development of a community market garden. I have spoken to Jean, the manager of the Community Centre, and she has talked to Mr Todd one of our directors. They both think it is a brilliant idea and suggested I present it to the directors at the next board meeting."

"It does sound like a really good idea Amelia, well done. Why don't you put the details of your plan together and I will present it to them for you? I am in the process of preparing the agenda of the meeting, you have timed it well."

"I am glad you like it Chloe. I feel so passionate about it and I would like to make the presentation myself. It will be a great opportunity for me to practise using Power Point. I know how keen you are to help us develop our IT skills and it would help me enormously to know you will be there to support me if I wobble a bit. I'm sure Jean would be happy to attend and explain how they could contribute to the project from the Community centre." Amelia held her breath as she waited for Chloe's response.

"You have obviously thought the project through very well and spoken to the right people," said Chloe coolly. "I congratulate you. I suggest you prepare your presentation and I will put it on the agenda under 'Future Developments.' We'll run through it together before the meeting to iron out any wrinkles."

"Odd Socks Ben is going to be so proud of me," Amelia whispered excitedly to herself as she went back to her desk. "I can't wait to see everyone next Tuesday."

They were all proud of her, as she was of their successes. There was a real buzz around the workshop that night.

"I knew you could do it Amelia." Ben said as he put his arm round her shoulders and gave her a friendly hug. Amelia could feel herself blushing from the top of her head to the bottom of her primly matching feet.

"Thanks Ben, I could not have done it without you and the rest of the group though."

Amelia found herself comparing Ben to Robert. Twice during the last week Robert had rung to cancel their date. Something important had cropped up at work – again! Hmm - someone, more likely, she had thought to herself. They had planned to go to the cinema on Saturday night, it was a film that Amelia especially wanted to see. On Saturday morning she decided to treat herself to a manicure and maybe buy something new to wear to celebrate her success at work. When she got back the phone was ringing. It was showing Robert's number.

"Hi Amelia, I'm really sorry but I will have to postpone our date yet again. Barry has had to back out of a dinner engagement with one of our senior partners and I have been asked to stand in for him. I said I didn't think you would mind." Amelia's cheeks flushed, this time with anger. How dare he take her so much for granted!

"Actually Robert, I do mind. This is the third time in a week you have let me down."

"I know and I have said I am sorry, haven't I? The film will be showing for the next two weeks at least. We can see it some other night can't we?"

"Yes, you are right Robert, I can see it another night but it won't be with you. There have been too many wasted evenings. I think I am worth better than the relationship you are offering me and it seems today is a good day to end it. Enjoy your dinner Robert."

As she slammed the phone down Amelia felt the tears starting to flow. Maybe she had spoken too quickly. Robert had been part of her life for a long time. Perhaps she should ring him back?

"I wish Debbie was here," she wailed, "and where's Odd Socks when I need him?" Just at that moment the doorbell rang. It was Debbie.

"Telepathy does exist," Amelia blurted and threw herself into her friend's arms.

"Whoa, what has happened?" Debbie gently stroked Amelia's back.

"It's all over between Robert and me."

"That's the best news I have heard in ages," Debbie exclaimed. "Listen to me Amelia, what is it they say? With every ending a new dawn arises – something like that! Come on, wash your face and get your running shoes on. You and I are going for a jog and then perhaps we'll call at The Crown and Anchor for a stiff drink. How does that sound?"

It didn't take long for Amelia to recognise that she had made the right decision, Robert had never been the right partner for her. As a couple they had been drifting along for far too long. When Tuesday evening finally arrived, Amelia was bubbling with excitement at the thought of telling her new friends what she had done. She especially wondered what Ben would think. This would be the last workshop and she felt sad to think the course was ending.

As she looked round the now familiar faces, Amelia realised good friendships had already begun. She was sure she would keep in touch with most of them, particularly Louise and Rachael. Both were so easy to get on with and she enjoyed their sense of humour. It had been so good witnessing their emergence from the self-doubt which had previously plagued them. Whatever happens, Amelia thought to herself, we have begun a new journey together. After the friendly greetings and a few minutes of light hearted chatter, they sat down. Ben stretched his legs in front of him, one blue and black ankle crossed casually over the green and white one, each looking quite at home with the other. Amelia smiled and when it was her turn to tell the group about her achievement, she adopted the same pose and casually crossed her pink and white ankle over its yellow partner.

"Robert is now part of my history!" she proudly proclaimed. The group cheered loudly.

"Well done Amelia, we all knew you could do it."

The workshop ended with arrangements being made to meet socially at The Crown and Anchor each week. Ben came over to Amelia.

"I like your socks," he said.

"Thanks, I've got another pair like these at home," she retorted cheekily. They grinned at each other.

"I am glad that you didn't go to the cinema with Robert. I would really like to see that film and I'm wondering if you and I could see it together?" Amelia was touched to see the anxious look in his eyes, despite the smile hovering round his lips.

"Yes, we could, I'd enjoy that Ben." They exchanged telephone numbers and arranged to meet outside the cinema the following Friday. Amelia practically skipped home, she felt so light hearted.

Thank goodness I bought that new top, it will be perfect for the occasion. She chuckled happily to herself as she picked up the phone to ring Debbie.

AMELIA'S SOCKS – A SOCKING TALE!
by Lavender Rose
(suitable to be read with younger children)

Baby Ben had been lying on his back in his play pen pulling his socks off. His big sister Amelia decided to copy him. She had just pulled one striped pink sock off, when Mum looked up from her knitting and asked if Amelia would like to read her new book. Amelia jumped up smiling and went to find her book.

Mum fed baby Ben and read while Amelia turned the pages. Then Amelia read to Mum making up a new, very exciting story. Mum took baby Ben upstairs to change his nappy and pop him in his cot for his nap. "When Grandad gets in we'll have a walk to the shop," said Mum, "you'll need both socks on Amelia, then I'll help you with your shoes."

Amelia went back to the front room to find her sock.

She looked on the floor and on the sofas - no sock.

She looked under the sofas - no sock.

She looked behind the sofa and behind the play pen - there was one…

It was baby Ben's red dinosaur sock.

Amelia tried to pull it on. It was very tiny and far too small.

Amelia put it in her pocket.

Amelia went to look in Mum and Dad's room.

She looked on the floor and on the bed - no sock.

She looked under the bed - no sock.

She looked behind the bed and behind the chest of drawers - there was one…

It was Mum's green trainer sock for the gym.

Amelia pushed her toes in, but it was big and baggy and soon fell off.

Amelia put it in her pocket.

Amelia went to look in the bathroom.

She looked on the floor and on the top of the wash basket - no sock.

She looked under the sink - no sock.

She looked behind the sink pipe and behind the wash basket - there was one…

It was Dad's light blue football sock with a dark blue top.

Amelia might have pulled it on. But it was very long and wet and muddy and very smelly!

Amelia carefully put it in her pocket.

Amelia went to look in the den.

She looked on the floor and on the desk - no sock.

She looked under the desk - no sock.

She looked behind the desk and behind the chair - there was one…

It was Grandad's grey bingo sock with lucky diamonds.

Amelia pulled it on. It was very big and had a hole in the toe.

Amelia took it off and put in her pocket.

Amelia went to look in her room. As soon as she went through the door she saw her pink spotty sock on the floor. Carefully she opened the top, put her toes inside and pulled it up.

Amelia looked down at her feet, smiled and wriggled her toes, she liked to wear odd socks.

Mum laughed when she saw Amelia's socks. "Maybe you'll start a new trend," said Mum.

That evening when Amelia was playing in her room she had a brilliant idea. Maybe she could start a trend…

She could hear that Mum was downstairs singing with Baby Ben. Dad was outside mowing the lawn and Grandad was snoring.

Amelia went into Mum and Dad's room. She knew Mum had two pairs of gym socks. Amelia looked in her sock drawer. Right at the back she spotted the white pair. She took one and put it in her other pocket.

She knew Dad had two pairs of football socks. Amelia looked in his sock drawer. Right in the middle she spotted the dark blue football socks with the light blue tops. She took one and put it in her other pocket.

Amelia crept into Grandad's room. Grandad went on snoring. She knew Grandad had two pairs of lucky bingo socks. Amelia looked in his sock drawer. Right at the front she spotted his grey bingo socks with lucky stars. Grandad went on snoring. She took one and put it in her other pocket.

Amelia crawled into Baby Ben's room. She knew Baby Ben had two pairs of dinosaur socks. Amelia looked in his bibs, vests and socks drawer. At the side she spotted his green dinosaur socks. She took one and put it in her other pocket.

The next day was Saturday. Amelia got ready by herself. She put on her clothes and with a smile she put on one pink stripy sock and one pink spotty sock.

She went downstairs.

Mum was wearing a green gym sock and a white gym sock. She wasn't smiling.

Dad was wearing a light blue football sock with a dark blue top and a dark blue football sock with a light blue top. He wasn't smiling.

Grandad was wearing a grey bingo sock with lucky diamonds and a grey bingo sock with lucky stars. He wasn't smiling.

Baby Ben was wearing a red dinosaur sock and a green dinosaur sock. He was lying on his back trying to pull them off. He was gurgling.

"I like odd socks," said Amelia.

"I don't," said Mum.

"I don't," said Dad.

"I don't," said Grandad.

"Gurgle," said Baby Ben.

"Maybe I could help you find some socks to match," said Amelia. "What would I get if I do?"

"AMELIA!" said Mum, Dad and Grandad, "Find those socks – NOW!"

"Gurgle," said Baby Ben.

To think about…

What do your favourite socks look like?

Where could Amelia have hidden all the socks?

Do you know anyone who wears odd socks? Why?

Draw a pair of socks. Are they odd socks? Who would wear them?

Who do you like to read with?

Do you read the words or use the pictures to make up stories?

Can you match your socks and roll the pairs together?

Do you keep your odd socks? If so, where?

ODD SOCKS *by Red Rose*

Amelia looked down at her feet,

Oh so pale and very petite.

Smiling she wiggled her toes,

And put on the rest of her clothes.

Always thinking outside of the box,

She decided to put on odd socks.

Picking two out of her drawer,

She sat herself down on the floor.

The red one was stripy and bright,

The blue one had hearts on in white.

What would mum say when she saw?

She shrieked when she'd worn them before!

Amelia looked down at her socks,

Then pulled on her steel toe capped Docs.

Chapter Four

"There are no strangers here; only friends you haven't yet met"

William Butler Yeats

Strangers

The real-life experience of one of the Roses – a stranger coming out of the door, provided endless possibilities for the writers. Powerful stories of lost love, tragedy and mistaken identity were cleverly created.

LENNY'S HOUSE *by Cornflower Rose*

I watched as the stranger came out of the front door and turned the lock. He couldn't see me but I could clearly see that he was carrying a large holdall, and looked very furtive. Who was he? He hoisted the bag over his shoulder and strode down the path, with his hoodie pulled low over his head, and walked away.

I was torn. Should I follow him or remain and wait until Old Lenny, the man who lived there, returned? I took my notepad out of my pocket and made a note of the time, adding a few extra descriptive details.

I decided to go with my gut instinct and started to follow the mystery man; making sure I was undetected and walking behind at a safe distance. I was feeling a bit apprehensive, as this was not the sort of thing I would normally do.

He turned right at the corner and continued down the road. I kept following, he kept walking.

I kept following for what seemed like ages. He came to a corner shop and went in. I waited outside and when he came out, I quickly turned and pretended to look at the window display. Out of the corner of my eye, I saw him take his mobile phone out of his pocket and make a call. He spoke for a little while, then put it back in his pocket. Quickly, I scribbled down this information into my notebook. He was now standing smoking a cigarette and reading a newspaper. This information also went into my notebook. I tried to remain inconspicuous, but it was getting dark and I was beginning to need a wee, and he just stood there. Things were getting desperate when I heard someone saying my name.

"Charlie Simpson what do you think you are doing?" Turning around I saw it was my Mum.

"Shushhh! Mum I'm undercover!" At that the mystery man put his paper into his holdall and came towards us. I started to tremble.

"Hello Mrs Simpson," he said.

"Oh! Dave, thanks for ringing me, sorry that you've been inconvenienced," she replied.

Laughing he said, "That's no problem, I have a young nephew and he likes to play the detective too."

"But Mum you don't understand, he's a robber. I saw him coming out of old Lenny's house with a big bag of swag."

"No Charlie, it's Dave, Len's son. Poor old Len's in hospital and Dave was collecting some things from his house to take to the hospital. He's not a robber."

"How was I to know that? He looks just like Robbery Bob on my computer game!"

"Charlie, you can't go around following people - playing at detective, and accusing them of all sorts. I think we are going to have to limit your time on the computer from now on."

And that was my first attempt at being a super sleuth detective. But I'm not giving up, there are lots of mysterious cases out there waiting to be solved... by me!

DESIGNS OF THE HEART   *by Jasmine Rose*

Stacy looked in the mirror and liked what she saw. A very attractive woman - smart, intelligent and successful - so what was wrong?

'You have a great social life and wonderful friends,' she told herself, but she knew, deep down, what was wrong - she was lonely. She missed her soul mate. With hindsight she recognised that Bill had once fulfilled that role, and she had spoiled the joy of what they had.

She had moved in with him three months after they met and they had been together for three and a half years. She was a student then, passionate about interior design. Bill had given her free range to try new ideas and colour schemes (no pink flowers in the bedroom of course!). He was a landscape gardener, just starting out in business, and between them they built a home which was innovative in style, yet emanated warmth and comfort inside and out. How happy they had been, perfect for each other. How could she have been so stupid and allowed their relationship to fall apart so easily? She had been too young and too selfish to appreciate all that he had offered her. She'd wanted more and Simon, her design tutor, had promised her all the things she had thought she needed - travel, glamour, excitement. What a trail they were going to blaze in the world of design!!

Bill was the only man she had ever really loved. He was kind, thoughtful, handsome and funny. He had loved her, oh how he had loved her. Stacy's heart sank as she thought back to the stricken look on his face when she told him she was leaving, moving away. "I can't believe you are doing this Stacy," he had said. "I love you so much, I can't even begin to imagine what life will be like without you."

That was six years ago, and she was a successful interior designer now, she was proud of her achievements. It hadn't taken long to realise the promises of glamour Simon had offered were as empty and shallow as he was. He had truly led her up the wrong garden path! Stacy realised what she had shared with Bill had been special. She knew that he still lived in the house they had shared (their house!). She longed to see him again and she also knew the next Design Fair she'd booked into was close to the village where they'd lived. She would practically pass the door!

As the weekend of the Fair drew near Stacy could barely contain her excitement. Her mind raced with thoughts of what might happen. If he would give her a second chance, she would do everything in her power to gain his trust and make him as happy as he'd been when they were together.

Friday finally arrived. Stacy dressed very carefully remembering that blue was Bill's favourite colour. She started her journey early to allow for any unforeseen traffic holdups. As she approached the village that had been her home, her heart was pounding. She decided to walk by the stream which ran through the village, to give herself some time to calm her nerves.

If she walked towards the house, maybe Bill would see her approaching. Would he open the door? As she came near to the gate, the door did open - her heart leapt and she held her breath! Seconds later a stranger came out and locked the door behind her.

"Mummy, can we go to see the beautiful new garden Daddy is making and surprise him while he is working?" said the little girl clutching the woman's hand. Stacy walked by, her knees buckling, feeling as if someone had hit her hard in her stomach.

She managed to walk back to the car, blinded by tears of disappointment. What was she doing? Did she honestly think she could just walk back into his life and pick up where they had left off! The tears rolled down her cheeks and she gasped for breath as she clambered into the car. There was a small consolation in knowing she hadn't made a fool of herself and Stacy took some comfort from that. Every muscle in her body was willing her to turn the car around and go home, but she knew she couldn't let her team down. They were a great bunch of people, each one talented in their own right; hardworking, dedicated, and best of all, so very loyal. Apart from the team, she owed it to herself, she had worked extremely hard to reach this point in her career and this Fair was her best chance to show how good a designer she had become! Taking a deep breath Stacy set her Sat Nav and drove to Crighton Hall where the fair was to be held. As she approached the Hall she was enchanted by the symmetry and style of this beautiful Georgian country house. It provided the perfect setting for her work. The clear, uncluttered lines of her furniture and soft furnishings would be complemented by the architecture of the building.

Her mood lifted, she was back in the zone! Work was her therapy and the heaviness in her heart shifted as she walked through the magnificent entrance to meet her team. She could see how the conservatory would provide the perfect setting for her designs and colour combinations. As they worked together the room soon mirrored the hues of the gardens beyond and, as the day progressed, house and garden each became an extension of the other, exactly as Stacy had intended. When all the finishing touches had been completed, the team stood back and surveyed their work, satisfaction 'writ large' on each face. Stacy was so proud of what they had accomplished together. "Thanks gang," she said, "a drink and a bite to eat is what we need now."

When they were seated round the table in the nearby restaurant, Stacy quietly absorbed the excitement and friendly banter flowing between her friends. The sound of their laughter was good. 'What a day of extremes,' she thought.

"Penny for them Stacy?" she heard Laura say.

She realised they were all looking at her, and Dave leaned over and gave her a hug. "Everything looks fantastic," he said. "This is going to be a very successful weekend."

Stacy smiled. "Thanks Dave, I am just thinking how lucky I am to have all of you supporting me." All six of them had opted to stay until the end of the event and, fortunately, they were all able to stay at the same hotel, which was not too far from the Hall. Only Ali knew about Bill and she was under strict orders not to tell anyone.

Stacy was the first to leave, all she wanted now was a hot bath then bed. It had been a long day in more ways than one.

"See you all in the morning, thank you for all your hard work today."

"Do you want me to walk with you?" asked Ali.

"No thanks Ali, not tonight, but it's good of you to ask." She gave them a warm smile, "Enjoy the rest of the evening."

Back in the hotel Stacy felt the turmoil of her emotions again. 'Oh Bill,' she thought. Despite her disappointment she wished him happiness, he deserved it. She wished with all her heart that it could have been her coming out of the house, holding their daughter's hand.

After a restless night, she managed to go down to breakfast with her friends.

"You look fantastic Stacy, so professional!"

'If only you knew how I feel,' she thought to herself. The short ride to Crighton helped to lift her spirits, just as it had done the day before. It was a beautiful day and boded well for her hopes to attract many new clients.

The team looked at their display with renewed pride.

"We're going to do well, I feel it in my bones," said Alex. He gave Stacy a big hug. "Well done boss!"

They did do well, lots of orders for soft furnishings and at least five clients wanting her to design the interior of their new conservatories or sun rooms. They all loved the idea of the house and garden being as one. Stacy was particularly proud of her reversible soft furnishings which could be turned as the seasons changed, maintaining the feeling of wholeness throughout the year.

One couple was especially keen for Stacy to visit their home as soon as possible.

"The builder has just finished and we really would love you to create this oneness, something unique to our home – it's brilliant! Will you be free to come to meet with the landscaping team on Tuesday? They have some great ideas for the garden and then you will be able to liaise with them, they promised to bring some initial plans." Stacy had wanted to get home as soon as possible on Monday. It would take most of the day to dismantle the display and they would all be tired. There was something about this couple though - maybe a good dose of their enthusiasm and excitement was just what she needed. She arranged to stay one more night at the hotel and to meet them at ten o'clock on Tuesday morning. By the time the visit was arranged, she was on first name terms with her clients - Maisie and Tim.

When the Fair came to an end, they were all tired but exhilarated, it had been a huge success. Stacy believed the orders they had taken would help to secure her company a place in the upper echelons of interior design. The future looked very promising indeed. If only she could be as fulfilled and successful in her private life as in her professional one!

Tuesday promised to be a good day for travelling - not too hot - and Stacy was pleased that Hoveton, the village where Maisie and Tim lived, was not far away. The visit should not take long and she had no trouble finding the house.

When she arrived, she saw that the gardeners were already parked on the drive, so she parked on the road in front of the house. Maisie had spotted her through the window and was already at the front door as Stacy walked up the path.

"Good timing Stacy, you're just in time to see the plans for the garden, hopefully they will help you with your designs for the sun room." She took Stacy through to the kitchen where Tim was poring over the plans with another man who had his back to them. Tim glanced up, "Stacy, it is good to see you! I'm glad you could find the time to come today. Mike, this is Stacy. Stacy, meet Mike, he is one of the partners in the landscaping company."

"Good to see you Stacy, Tim and Maisie have been telling me about your work. It sounds fabulous."

Maisie made a cup of tea and, in no time at all, the four of them were engrossed in the designs for the garden. Stacy could feel herself being drawn into the planning discussion. She could see loads of opportunities to incorporate her latest designs into the interior of the house. A clever use of mirrors and textiles would give Maisie and Tim exactly what they hoped to achieve. When Stacy finally remembered to look at her watch, she realised she would have to get a move on if she was to meet with her team today. She promised to bring her ideas on paper for their next meeting. As she was about to leave, they heard a car door slam and footsteps running around the side of the house.

"Daddy, Daddy!" a voice shouted and a little girl hurtled around the corner, through the open door and hurled herself at Mike. "Guess who picked me up from nursery!"

"Was it Mummy? asked Mike.

"No," she said, but before she could say who the mystery person was, he was already standing in the doorway. Stacy's heart stood still! She had recognised the little girl - last seen on Friday, outside Bill's door!

Mike scooped his daughter up and turned to Stacy, "Hannah, say hello to Stacy," then he turned back to face the door. "Thanks for picking Hannah up Bill. Come and meet Stacy, it looks as though we are going to be working together in the near future, she has some great ideas for the interior of the sun room." He turned back to Stacy, "Bill's not just a partner, he's just about the best mate a bloke could have. Putting up with the three of us until we find a house we like is no mean feat - especially with little Miss Mischief here!" he laughed.

Stacy couldn't move! Her eyes locked into Bill's, her heart was now hammering so fast she could scarcely hear what Mike was saying. She willed herself to take a step forward, aware of the bemused glances between Maisie, Tim and Mike.

"Bill," she stammered, "it is so good to see you." She held out her hand. She could see that his colour had paled underneath the weathered tan of his unforgettably handsome face, but his hand was steady as he held hers. She turned to the others, everyone seemed lost for words! "I really have to dash but I'll see you soon."

"How long this time?" asked Bill gently.

"Two weeks," she replied.

"Two weeks, I think I can manage that." As he walked her to the car they heard the others talking.

"What was all that about?" Tim exclaimed. "Did you put something in the tea Maisie?"

"If you did, I'd better be going!" Mike chuckled.

"If you did, I'll have another cup!" retorted Tim and they burst out laughing.

Stacy and Bill smiled, there was so much to be said and no time to say it. "Can I ring you Stacy?"

"I'd like that," she said, "I'd like that very much." She knew from the look in his eyes that their future would take root and not just in Maisie and Tim's garden!

THE PARTY

by Lavender Rose

(suitable to be read with younger children)

What's going on? What's the score?
Everyone's at the wrong door!

John lives at number one,
The person's wrong leaving number one.

Sue lives opposite at number two.
Exiting two, who are you?

Why is Lee at number three?
Three is not his place to be.

Who's that at number four?
Four is really not her door!

What about Clyve at number five?
That's not where he should arrive.

Things must be in such a mix,
If Vic's over at number six.

I will say it with expression,
Evan doesn't live at seven.

Is that Kate standing at the gate?
Her home is not at number eight.

Why are you at number nine?
That house is Mum's and mine!

With new friends we'll party at ten,
Then return to our right homes again.

To think about...

Sing your favourite number songs.
Who lives in your house?
Can you make up some number rhymes of your own?

THE RUINED FRANGIPANES *by Red Rose*

As I passed his door a stranger came out and turned the lock. Adorning his head was a straw boater with a striped band, shading his eyes from the sun. He passed me by with a spring in his step as I slowed down with the pretence of admiring the begonias in the vicar's garden. I never gave him a second thought as I strolled on home to pick up the frangipanes I had baked that morning, ready for the summer fete.

My plan was to go to the church hall an hour earlier to help the vicar set out the tables ready for the cake stalls. Humming contentedly I made my way there, enjoying the sunshine on my face and letting my thoughts run away with me. I was looking forward to spending some time alone with Vicar John. We were quite familiar, on first name terms with each other now. I quite fancied myself as a vicar's wife, and we got on so well, he always waxed lyrical about my baking and had a weakness for my frangipane tarts.

I arrived at the Church hall and let myself in. There was no sign of him but the sound of furniture scraping across the wooden floor filtered out from the kitchen. "Ahh, he must be moving the tables." Tenderly taking the lid off the Tupperware container I exposed my perfectly formed frangipanes ready for the vicar's approval; this was my best batch yet. Making my way over to the kitchen, I peered wide eyed through the half open door.

It took a few seconds to register what I was seeing. There was Vicar John, *my* Vicar John, against the table in the arms of the stranger who was now bare-chested, the straw boater strewn on the floor along with his shirt. The bottom fell out of my world and simultaneously the box of frangipanes slipped out of my clutches, clattering to the floor.

Both men jumped, aghast as they saw me standing there, open mouthed. Red faced Vicar John quickly untangled himself from the clinch and his mouth slackened, "Betty you startled us. This is my good friend Robert."

An ache started deep in my chest as my lips trembled, "Nice to meet you Robert." I bent down to pick up the frangipanes as Robert bent down to pick up his shirt.

Chapter Five

"All that we see or seem is but a dream within a dream"

Edgar Allan Poe

Was It a Dream?

Dreaming is something we all do. It's the only time our subconscious flies unhindered. Here our stories introduce characters in challenging situations. Will their hopes and desires be fulfilled?

THE WHITE FEATHER *by Cornflower Rose*

I had that dream again the other night, the same as the night before. I was standing in a garden, but not just any garden, this one was in high definition – like technicolour in the movies. Vibrant colours with amazing exotic looking plants, flowers and shrubs surrounding me. It was the most wondrous sight. I had a sense of aloneness whilst walking amongst the fabulous displays which included roses of every hue; blue, red, yellow, pink, purple and white and all in full, resplendent bloom. I reached out and touched the silk soft petals and they cascaded to the ground at my feet and emitted a scent so rich and aromatic I was compelled to pick one up and put it in my pocket.

'I must be in heaven,' I remember thinking. Then another thought occurred to me – 'if I am in heaven then maybe I will see my mother here?' The most wonderful feeling of joy, elation and hope filled my heart. I'd never felt such an encompassing feeling of contentment before.

I continued with my ramble through the garden, smiling in my euphoria. Each step took me deeper into the garden and the flora all around was looking more glorious as I went, but I never met a soul. It eventually dawned on me that there was no sign of my mother, but at the same time I had a strange feeling that her presence was close. I had mixed emotions; feeling disappointed and bereft but at the same time seeming comforted by the fact she was near. I had missed her so much.

So, imagine my surprise on leaving the house next morning and seeing a small, pure white feather floating down and landing on my doorstep. I stooped and tenderly picked it up and put it in my pocket. As I did so I unexpectedly felt a piece of paper in the corner of the pocket and puzzled, I pulled it out. It was folded into a very small square. It had familiar looking hand writing on the front. I unfolded the sheet of paper and read the following:

I placed a feather on your path,

Small, white and whole.

A sign so you will think of me,

Its purpose to console.

I know it will comfort you,

When you're troubled and sad,

That's why I've sent to you this sign,

So you won't feel so bad.

I smiled to myself and my heart leapt with joy. I just knew my mother was still thinking of me, even though she couldn't physically be with me.

Was it possible that the heavenly petal I placed in my pocket in my dream manifested into the note from my mother? I chose to believe so.

Feeling contented and comforted I carried on about my day, looking forward to another heavenly dream that night.

Of Prose and Pen

JENNY'S DREAM *by Jasmine Rose*

For a long time, Jenny's waking hours had been spent thinking back to her life as it was before the accident. She was so fit and she could run like the wind - that was how it felt when she was running freely. She never forgot that feeling.

Her P.E. teacher at school thought she showed real promise, so she joined the local running club. The trainers there thought she showed lots of promise too and it wasn't long before Jenny was representing school and club at local and regional athletic meetings, winning prizes and trophies. She loved it! The long hours of training were no problem, because that was all she wanted to do.

It seems ironic that the accident happened on her way to the running club. She was late and dashed, without thinking, across the road, behind the bus. The driver of the car didn't stand a chance as she ran in front of him. The medical staff at the hospital were wonderful - they saved her life. Sadly, they were not able to save her foot.

Gradually, Jenny learned to walk again. The prosthesis felt awkward and clumsy at first but she managed to get used to it. She still had that streak of determination in her! Life was almost normal again, but she couldn't run. At that time she thought her heart would never mend because that was what she loved to do more than anything in the world.

Every night, she dreamed of running - sometimes she could even hear her club mates cheering her on as she raced to victory, then she would wake with a start and she knew she had been dreaming. Jenny knew nothing about the para-athletic movement then.

All of that seemed such a long time ago. So much had happened since. When she woke this morning she thought back to yesterday. She relived the excitement of the day. She could feel the adrenalin pumping through her body, her eyes were fixed on the finishing line. She was running like the wind and the crowds were cheering her on. Suddenly her alarm went off, shattering her reverie! She sat up with a start, 'was that a dream?' Jenny turned quickly to her dressing table and heaved a sigh of relief. She reached out and picked up her medal. This was real and now she had a new dream – next time the medal would be gold.

WINGS AND THINGS *by Lavender Rose*
(suitable to be read with slightly older children)

"Helllllp!" came the faint cry again. I looked for ages before I realised where the sound was coming from. My Nan had always said there were fairies at the bottom of the garden, but we never believed her. But here was a delicate, beautiful, tiny, person-like, winged creature that could talk. Only her dirt smeared top half was showing. The rest of her was completely stuck in the mud. Her wings were buzzing furiously and she was trying to grasp blades of grass to pull herself out. She was slowly sinking in the brown, oozy slime. She said she had dropped her magic wand which would have been her best way of escaping such a sticky situation. Neither of us could see it.

But being big meant it was easy to help. I squatted down. Carefully I held out my finger for her to wrap her arms around, then slowly pulled my hand back as she gradually eased herself out.

She said her name was Ederone, and she wished she could stay and be my friend, but she had a very important fairy meeting to go to. We searched and searched and found the muddy magic wand and she was able to magic herself clean and ready. But before she left she said I deserved a reward.

She gave me my very own set of fairy wings that really worked! I just had to wish them in place on my back and they would appear and stay until I was in a safe place and wished them away again.

Ederone made me promise that I wouldn't tell anyone my wonderful secret. She warned me that if I did the wings would disappear completely and I would only remember them in my dreams. If anyone saw my wings and realised they were real, they would only remember what they had seen in their dreams too.

Showing them off wasn't allowed. Not if I wanted to keep my wings. So, I had to be careful, I had to watch out, that there was no-one about when I tried them out.

The wings looked quite like the ones we played with when I went to nursery. Their's were gold and shiny and had elastic that went over my shoulders. But these were special… they stayed on even when I flew.

At first it was hard learning to fly.

I went too fast. I hit a tree trunk.

I went too slow. I landed on my bottom.

I went too high. I realised I might be seen.

I went zig-zag. I did a crazy double somersault in the air.

But soon I got the hang of it and could whizz and flit safely. It was easier than learning to roller skate or ride my bike and it was sooooooooo much fun. But being seen wasn't allowed. Not if I wanted to keep my wings. So, I had to be careful, I had to watch out, that there was no-one about when I tried them out.

I spent a lot of time flying round my bedroom. I didn't have much time for the usual reading my books at bedtime. Instead I practised going up and down, forwards and backwards, making circles and loops in all directions. Normally if I get up my grown-ups can hear the bed groaning and the floor boards squeaking. But if I managed gentle take-offs and landings, there was nothing to hear. My wings were very quiet unless you got up close – and of course that wasn't allowed. Not if I wanted to keep my wings. So, I had to be careful, I had to watch out, that there was no-one about when I tried them out.

One day I heard sad cheeping from the tree at the bottom of our back garden. There was a nest with four hungry blackbird chicks. Mr. Blackbird had a problem. He had found lots of juicy worms, but had hurt his beak on a stone and was finding it hard to carry the squirmy worms to his babies. Mrs. Blackbird was worn out doing all the work. I checked the coast was clear. Spotting my wings wasn't allowed. Not if wanted to keep my wings. So, I had to be careful, I had to watch out, that there was no-one about when I tried them out.

I wished on my special wings and flew up and down with wriggling worms in my fingers. I didn't really like it, but our blackbird family was very happy. Then, when the chicks were two weeks old they were ready to fledge and we were soon practicing flying together.

A few days later I heard the lady next door crying. She was standing near the fence. When I asked her what was up, she explained that she had lost the locket that her children had bought for her a long time ago. It had their pictures in and was extra special because they had saved their pocket money to buy it. She reckoned it would turn up in the garden somewhere, but hoped it would turn up soon.

I checked there wasn't anyone near 'cos revealing my wings wasn't allowed. Not if I wanted to keep my wings. So, I had to be careful,

I had to watch out, that there was no-one about when I tried them out.

I wished on my wings and flew all around her garden looking for the locket and chain's sparkle. I couldn't see anything. Then I heard Mr. and Mrs. Magpie screeching in their nest. I remembered what my Nan had said about magpies being collector maniacs. I'd wait till they were away from the nest and then have a peek. I was glad I had. Along with bits of wool and plastic wrappers, were a pair of glasses, a shiny cake case and there was a gold chain and a gold locket. Carefully I took them out and dropped them near the front door, to be easy for her to find.

Another day the boy next door at the other side was outside playing with five beanbags. He threw one so high it landed on his garage roof. I heard him cry and could see the problem. While he went inside to get his dad I did a quick check. My wings being noticed wasn't allowed. Not if I wanted to keep my wings. So, I had to be careful, I had to watch out, that there was no-one about when I tried them out

I quickly wished on my wings, and up I flew. I dropped the beanbag off the side of the roof. I gently flew down and landed in my garden just as I heard their kitchen door creak open. At the same time my big brother came out of their house.

"What were you up to? I was sure I saw you flying …

   … in my dream last night!" were the first words he said to me at breakfast the next morning.

Funny, I had that dream too!

WAS IT JUST A DREAM? *by Red Rose*

Cassie awoke to the sunlight streaming in through a crack in the curtains. Arms outstretched she felt the empty space beside her with a mixture of trepidation and relief. Eyes squinting she leaned over and grasped her old mobile phone, her heart racing as she turned it on... hundreds of missed calls and too many texts to count.

Was it just a dream, did she imagine it? Plumping her pillows she propped herself up, then cast her mind back to yesterday and the events that had been painstakingly planned and carried out with military precision. Everything had to be just as normal. She had barely slept the night before, lying rigid in their bed willing the dawn to arrive. The welcome sound of Graham's alarm finally came at 6am and they started their usual morning routine.

She got up first, showered and put on without question the plain underwear, black trousers and high-necked blouse he had picked out for her the night before, then went down to prepare breakfast while he showered.

As they sat down to eat he studied her face intently, it was scrubbed bare of make-up, just the way he liked it. With a look of satisfaction, he said, "Your lips are dry Cassie." He walked over to the bureau then unlocked it. "Here, put this on," passing her some clear lip salve. She applied it sparingly not wanting to antagonise him as he watched, then she placed it back into his outstretched hand.

He returned it to the bureau, next to the few items of make-up he allowed her to wear when he felt it was appropriate, then picked up her mobile phone. It was a 'Pay as you Go' old Nokia without any credit. A new phone would be wasted on her he said, she didn't need internet access he said. She held her breath as he frowned while checking it for messages, "Your damn cousin again, wanting to pop over for coffee...can't she take a hint?" He passed her the phone. "If she rings, ignore it." Cassie nodded as she put the phone in her bag.

She followed the usual routine of washing the breakfast dishes while he checked his emails and prepared his briefcase ready for the day ahead.

He was ready before her, his eyes narrowed as he scoured the kitchen. She held her breath as his face stiffened when he spotted the two mugs left on the drainer. "Cassie!" he bellowed, his face like thunder. She tried to remain calm as his fist came down with a thump on the worktop, "Can't you do just one thing right!" Quaking inside she rushed over and opened the cupboard putting them in the correct spot, making sure the handles pointed to the right.

His mood had changed, anger bristled from him. "Useless bitch!" he spat as he grabbed his briefcase. She knew to remain silent as she put on her jacket, picked up her bag and followed him outside, waiting while he locked the door behind him. They sat in silence as he drove her to work. She was a Sales Assistant in a high-end clothes shop. She adored her job, it was her sanctuary and escape, it was the only interaction she had with other people apart from him.

His face softened as they pulled up outside, "See you later sweetheart." He leaned over and cupped her face kissing her cheek. "You know I love you. Remember today is the day I have my annual meeting with the shareholders so I won't be ringing you till 12.30. Make sure you answer the phone when I call, you know it upsets me if you don't."

She smiled and followed her script, the empty meaningless words, the words she tells him every day, the words he wants and needs to hear. "Of course darling, I love you too."

As he watched, she got out of the car trying to walk as if everything was a normal day. He sat outside with the engine running for what seemed like an age to Cassie, with his usual routine of gazing into the shop window watching her while she took off her jacket. Her insides were churning as she started to get the shop ready for opening.

When he finally drove off Pam came rushing out from the backroom. "Has he gone Cassie? Right! Action Stations!" Grabbing Cassie's jacket, she beckoned her into the changing room and gave her a holdall, containing; a new phone, toiletries and clothes (luckily they were the same size).

"Mike is parked at the backdoor. Are you ready to go?" Mike was Pam's husband and a Computer Technician. They were the only real friends she had left in the world. Graham had managed to drive everyone else away.

"I'm scared Pam, but yes... if I don't do it now I never will."

She handed Mike her mobile phone as she got into the car and he changed the settings to make sure she couldn't be tracked before they set off.

And that's how she ended up here, in this hotel room, on her own, away from the manipulation, fear and control of the husband who had ground her down into half the woman she'd been before. She recognised this now, it had taken much heartache and many painful hours for her to finally come to realise that the problem lay with him, not her.

Turning over she felt under the pillow, pulling out the scratch card her and Pam had bought from the tips left by their lovely customers. It was a winning ticket, £50,000. At first they couldn't believe their eyes, but it was true. £25,000 each, it was enough to set her up somewhere else. A new start she thought as her old Nokia started flashing again with his number. Ignoring it she clambered out of bed and walked over to the holdall taking out the new iPhone and bag of make-up Pam had packed for her.

Sitting down at the dressing table she emptied out the contents. Looking at herself in the mirror she savoured the luxury of applying two layers of Rose Pink lip gloss, then looked down at her old phone and half smiled as she whispered, "Goodbye Graham," and turned it off for the very last time.

Chapter Six

"No sign, so far, of anything sinister - but I live in hope"

Agatha Christie

- Cat Among the Pigeons

Who's That?

'Looking at the photo she wondered who was the sinister looking man standing behind her mother…'

Thought provoking storylines, from very different angles. The stories in this chapter feature a variety of diverse ideas: journeys into destiny, deception, dark intentions and budding detectives.

SUSPICION *by Cornflower Rose*

Ellie heard the ping on her phone. Looking at it, she hoped it was from her mum. It was a notification from Facebook, smiling she opened her account.

Yes, at last, there was a post from her mum. She'd been quite concerned when her widowed mum, at the age of 72, had decided to go on an extended holiday to the other side of the world with her best friend Edna. Considering their ages, they were both fit, fun-loving go-getters, who loved to try new challenges. So far, they had travelled around Australia, New Zealand and Tasmania. Now they were in Thailand after visiting Cambodia and Vietnam. Before leaving on the trip of a lifetime, Ellie had insisted Anne, her mum, keep in touch with Facebook and Instagram, both excellent media for that purpose.

Ellie loved receiving the messages and photos and, as promised, she had them all stored into folders in chronological order on her computer, ready for her mum to access when she eventually arrived home.

Opening today's offerings, taken in Phuket there were splendid shots of scenery with Anne and Edna in various poses, clearly having the time of their lives. Amongst the selfie photos and scenery pictures, there was one of a group which had the pair of them centre front. Everyone was smiling and waving at what looked like a beach party. Ellie was happy that her mum was having such a wonderful time, but also missing her and looking forward to her returning home soon. Looking at the photo she wondered who was that sinister looking man standing behind mum? An uneasy feeling came over her. Zooming in and enlarging the frame she could see that his eyes, instead of looking front for the camera, were actually focused on Anne. The wry smile on his face reinforced her concern. His looks could only be described as dark and brooding. Perhaps, she thought, I've been reading too many mystery novels, but there was just something that caught her attention; she felt like she had seen him somewhere before.

Clicking back through her mum's photo collection, she paid more attention to the detail.

Sure enough on inspecting the photos, in some guise or other, was the same man. Always in the background never at the fore. It was like he was stalking her. Opening previous folders, she spotted him in every location at some point. What could this mean? Mum had never mentioned any romantic attachment and, if there was, surely they would have been seen together?

How come he appeared to be there at every destination? Panicking, she thought: what if he was out to harm her mum in some way? After her father had passed away, Anne became a wealthy woman, hence being able to afford this very expensive, luxury holiday for her and Edna. She was a magnet for any free-loader wanting a meal ticket.

Going back to the latest picture she zoomed in on his face and enlarged it as much as she could without distorting it, then saved it onto her iPad. She didn't want to worry her mum but she felt she had to speak to her without raising any suspicions. She needed to ascertain whether she knew him. Skype seemed the easiest way, so she set up a call.

Anne and Edna were in their hotel room after having their lunch. They were relaxed and content, and very pleased to hear from Ellie. After the preliminary pleasantries, Ellie asked a few discreet questions, and it became clear that neither Anne, nor Edna knew any of the people in their group photo. It was taken by a holiday rep at an organised beach party.

Feeling sick in the pit of her stomach she decided to email her friend Lucy, she needed to talk to someone about her fears. Attaching the photo to a message she explained to Lucy about this guy in the background of her mum's photos. Lucy worked for an organisation that specialised in Heir Hunting and Ellie hoped she might have an idea of what steps to take to find out his identity and perhaps relay her fears.

Lucy replied sometime later and promised to look at the information and speak to a few of her colleagues to see if they had any suggestions.

It was nerve wracking for Ellie waiting to hear back from Lucy, but when she did it was not what she wanted to hear. Apparently, Lucy's boss Greg had a contact at a Tracing Agency who locate people in the UK and Overseas. He'd passed on the photo and inquired if he knew this guy's identity. Within 24 hours Greg had received a reply. The man in question, a Rupert Smythe, was wanted by Interpol for serious fraud in the UK and attempted murder. Apparently, he was a known womaniser who had cheated three unsuspecting elderly females out of their life savings and was a possible suspect for attempted murder. His modus operandi was to identify his victim, by looking through obituary columns in local newspapers and internet searches. He would then try to isolate his victim from family and friends, make his move to ingratiate himself, gain their trust and then cheat them out of their savings. It looked as if, so far, he hadn't managed to seduce her mother.

Ellie's heart nearly stopped beating! She could only presume that he was biding his time for an opportunity to separate Anne from Edna, so that he could work his charm then swindle her out of her fortune, or worse, kill her!

She must get hold of her mum immediately to alert her and demand she cut short her holiday and return home.

Disregarding the time difference, she rang her mum's number. It rang out, eventually going to voicemail. She tried again. This time it was picked up and Edna answered, saying Anne was sleeping as she had a migraine, and asking what was so urgent at this time of night?

Quickly, Ellie explained her dilemma. Edna listened patiently, then told her to calm down, she already knew everything about the man.

She explained to Ellie that she had worked for MI5 when she was young, so was well versed in surveillance and she knew the protocol when suspecting a potential crime was to be committed. Edna reassured her that they were being protected and the fraudster was going to be picked up by police on their arrival back in Australia. Anne was unaware of any of this, but Edna had known he was following them, and if everything went to plan, the police would get their man.

She urged Ellie to stay calm and not to worry her mum, as she wanted her to enjoy the rest of her holiday in blissful ignorance and they would be home soon. One other thing she said to Ellie was that she was impressed with her deduction skills and that she'd do well to enrol in the Intelligence Agency as they could use people like her.

Relieved that everything was in hand and that her mum was safe with Edna, she thought maybe she'd consider Edna's suggestion, and felt a new career looming, all thanks to her mum's zest for life.

MAN OF MYSTERY *by Jasmine Rose*

The last two weeks had brought a rollercoaster of emotions for Margaret as she sifted through her mother's belongings. A real, 'This is Your Life,' experience, brought to her through photographs, letters and personal possessions. The boxes might have stayed unopened forever, stacked in her spare room, if it hadn't been for the letter from her Australian niece, Sandie.

Sandie was now well enough to travel and wanted to come to England next month. Could she stay with Margaret and Johnny? She had been devastated at not being able to attend her grandma's funeral as she'd been recovering from surgery. She had really wanted to be there to support Margaret.

"Of course, she must stay with us," Johnny said as he read the letter, "a visit from Sandie will do us both good. It will be great to see her." They arranged for their daughters, Amy and Laura, to come around the next Saturday to help

Margaret sort through their grandma's belongings. Once that was done the spare room could be made ready for Sandie's visit. They decided to put all the old photographs in a separate folder for Margaret and Sandie to look through together. Maybe Sandie would be able to help Margaret to put names to those faces she didn't recognise.

"It's so frustrating to think that these people are our own flesh and blood and we don't even know what their names are," said Amy. "Why didn't they write them on the back of the photographs when they were printed?"

"Do you do that?" her dad asked her, a wry smile on his face.

"No," she admitted with a little giggle. "Anyway, it's all digital now, things are different." They laughed and continued with the task.

"I think Amy is right," said Laura, as she fished a group photograph out of a box. "I wonder who this sinister chap is standing behind you Mum?"

"Blimey!" said Amy as she peered over Laura's shoulder, "That's a face that has never had a smile living in it!" Margaret looked at the photograph.

"This was taken just before Sandie's mum, your Aunt Isobel, emigrated to Australia She and Uncle Michael had only been married a couple of weeks and your grandma and grandpa decided to have a big family party, including all those who didn't come to the wedding. Isobel was only nineteen and I was twelve. I really missed her for a long time after she left."

"I don't remember everyone who was at the party but perhaps Sandie can help us? I'm sure my sister would have shown her any photographs and talked about them often. I'm pretty sure your grandma sent the negatives and copies of all the photographs to Isobel. She must have thought that this could be the last time she would see the whole of the extended family together."

It was finally the day of Sandie's arrival, Amy and Laura went with Margaret and Johnny to the airport to meet her.

"It's so wonderful to see you," Margaret said as she hugged her niece, "you must be worn out? Let's get you home."

Margaret hadn't made any plans for the next couple of days, she felt it only fair to allow

Sandie time to recover from her long journey. Her son Andrew and his family were coming down from Scotland at the weekend. He was really looking forward to seeing his cousin, so the whole family would be together then.

On the day after her arrival Sandie and Margaret were sitting in the garden enjoying the sunshine.

"We've finally sorted out your grandma's belongings," said Margaret, "I'd like you to have her pearl necklace. She wanted you to have it too. She remembered how much you admired it when you visited last time. We also put aside a box of old family photographs. I thought you might be able to help me to put a name to some of the people in them. I know your mum was always keen to keep you informed of who was who in the extended family. She didn't want you to forget your English roots!"

"Let's look at them now," Sandie responded, "it'll be nice for the two of us, to take a little journey back in time together."

Margaret brought the box from the house and they reminisced as they looked through the contents. Aunts, uncles and distant cousins were brought to mind and they remembered anecdotes and stories about each one.

"Do you know who this chap is?" Margaret asked as she picked up the photograph her daughters had found previously.

"I've no idea." Sandie replied after she had studied the photo. "Maybe he was a friend of Grandma and Grandpa. He doesn't look very happy, poor man! There were so many people there that day, I don't think even Ma could remember them all. She always said that Rose Cottage was a lovely house to grow up in. She loved the freedom of the big garden. That is where you were all standing when you had the photograph taken wasn't it? Mind you," Sandie went on to say, "Ma always said there was a bit of a dark history allegedly attached to the house. Something had happened before Grandma and Grandpa bought it. She never went into any detail, all I know is that she was happy there."

"Yes, we were," said Margaret. "We were sad when we had to move further north for Dad's work."

"Why don't we drive down there to see if it is still there?" Sandie blurted. Aunt and niece looked excitedly at each other.

"What a great idea," Margaret responded. "We could stay overnight, somewhere close, then we can take our time driving back. We could visit a few childhood haunts on the way. We'll have an adventure!"

The family were delighted when their mum and Sandie told them what they were planning for the last week of Sandie's stay.
"Good for you," said Andrew who had just arrived from Scotland.

Amy said she would look on the Internet for a good hotel. "It will be our treat," she said. Laura and Andrew agreed.

Johnny declined the invitation to go with them. "I'm sure you'll have much more fun without me tagging along," he said jovially.

"I wonder what the dark history was?" proffered Laura.

"Yes, I'm intrigued by that?" Andrew said, "In fact I think I will do a bit of digging when I go to my genealogy group on Monday night. We meet at our local library and we have access to old newspaper articles using the microfiche. Maybe I'll find some clues which will lead to a story. Gosh! Maybe there is a skeleton in the family cupboard after all!"

"Whatever happened was before Aunt Mags and Ma's time there, but it would be interesting to find out?" Sandie commented.

A few days before they were due to go, a letter arrived from Andrew.

Dear Mum and Sandie,
I thought you might be interested in the enclosed newspaper article which I retrieved from the archives, The Yorkshire Observer to be precise.
Enjoy your trip!
Love Andrew

The headline on the enclosed sheet of paper jumped out at them as they unfolded it:

Local Man Acquitted of Wife's Murder

Mr. John Dunstable, 47, of Rose Cottage, Flitworth, Yorkshire was yesterday found to be not guilty of his wife's murder due to lack of sufficient evidence.

Mrs. Dunstable was reported missing last September following a violent row with her husband. Neighbours,

concerned for her safety, had reported the incident to the police. They said they had heard Mr. Dunstable threatening his wife on the evening of her disappearance. They also reported that they had seen bruising on her face several times during the months before the incident.

A bloodstained log had been discovered beneath a hedge close to the cottage garden. Mrs. Dunstable has never been found.

Next to the article was a photograph of John Dunstable standing outside of Rose Cottage. Margaret and Sandie gasped when they saw it – this was the same man who stood behind Margaret in the family photograph!

"How could Mum and Dad have invited him?" Margaret whispered.

"They didn't," said Johnny, "look at the date when the article was published." They looked to the top of the page where Andrew had written, 11th June 1918, fifty-six years before the photograph was taken!

"That is so spooky!" gasped Sandie. "Do you still want to go Aunt Mags?"

"Yes, I do," she replied, "I think we should."

They visited Rose Cottage as planned. It looked beautiful, just as Margaret remembered it with the roses, in full bloom, climbing up the wall round the front entrance. Using their new iPad's, they even managed to take photographs of themselves, standing beside the garden gate.

The church stood at the other end of the village and they made their way to the churchyard. Andrew had also furnished them with the knowledge that John Dunstable had continued to live in the village after the trial until his death in 1939, aged 68 years. He had always professed himself to be innocent of his wife's murder.

As they meandered slowly through the churchyard, they eventually found what they were searching for - John Dunstable's headstone.

"Well done!" they said to each other. Margaret bent down and scooped a small patch of grass away. She put the likeness of the man, which she had cut from the photo, in the earth underneath, then replaced the grass and covered it with a small bunch of roses.

"We'll never know whether he did it or not," she said. "Maybe his wife left him and made a new life for herself."

"I hope so," Sandie responded. "One thing for sure - I bet this is the first time anyone ever brought him flowers!"

When Sandie returned home, she skyped Margaret. "I found Ma's photograph of the family group," she said and held it up for Margaret and Johnny to see.

They looked closely and could see no sign of John Dunstable.

WHO'S THAT IN THE PHOTO? *by Lavender Rose*
(suitable to be read with younger children)

There's Mum in the photo,

But…

   behind her looking scary,

Who can that be?

It's just Uncle Morris, reaching for his key.

There's Uncle Morris in the photo,

But…

   under the table looking hungry,

Who can that be?

It's just Mischief the Dog, begging for her tea.

There's Mischief the Dog in the photo,
But...
    next to her looking upset,
Who can that be?
It's just Baby Moses, who's hurt his knee.

There's Baby Moses in the photo,
But...
    on the chair hissing, looking angry,
Who can that be?
It's just Molly the Cat, chasing a bee.

There's Molly the Cat in the photo,
But...
    dashing past looking desperate,
Who can that be?
It's just Grandad Monty, who needs a wee.

There's Grandad Monty in the photo,

But...

    in front of him looking puzzled,

Who can that be?

It's just Aunt Mary, who dropped a pea.

There's Aunty Mary in the photo,

But...

    beside her looking happy,

Who can that be?

With a big smile on my face – IT'S JUST ME!

To think about...

Can you act out all the characters' feelings?
What other feelings can you act out?
What letter does each characters' name begin with?
Talk about the people you know and the things they do, can you draw the photos?
Say more words that rhyme with be, key, tea...

ABIGAIL *by Red Rose*

Looking at the photograph that had been placed on the chest of drawers next to her bed, Abigail wondered who the sinister looking man could be standing behind her mother.

Abigail was only thirteen and her sister Grace eleven when their mother had died five years ago, and they both still missed her terribly.

Turning away she walked over to the window and gazed out at the all familiar view, taking in each and every detail of their beautiful garden and fields beyond. It truly was a magical place to live, and they had been so lucky to enjoy such a privileged childhood growing up here.

She looked towards the door startled as she heard hushed voices coming from the landing. At that moment her beloved collie dog bounded into the room then turned and stood in the doorway, omitting a low growl as if on guard.

"What's wrong Jasper? Come on boy," but he didn't flinch. This was all very odd, something was not quite right. She could hear wailing coming from downstairs, it sounded like her sister Grace.

She felt uneasy as if something had happened, but she couldn't quite remember what it was. Jasper carried on growling menacingly at the door. Abigail looked down at her bare feet peeping out from under her white nightgown and felt a bit cold, she would lie down for a while.

Making her way back over to the bed she gasped as she noticed someone else staring out from the photograph, it was a young woman holding the sinister man's hand. She started to tremble, she recognised the man now, it was Uncle Harold her mother's brother, and the young woman...? No! How could this be?

The confusion left as realisation dawned, and her whole soul started to shake as her gaze turned to the bed and looked down upon a lifeless young body. It was her, she was looking down at herself. She was dead!

Jasper bared his teeth as he sensed Uncle Harold entering the room, Abigail knew now why her dog was behaving like this, he didn't want her to go, he wanted her here with him. Jasper whimpered as she kissed him goodbye, then she tentatively took hold of Uncle Harold's outstretched hand and set off on her new journey...

Chapter Seven

"Every impulse of feeling should be guided by reason; and, in my opinion, exertion should always be in proportion to what is required"

Jane Austen

- *Pride and Prejudice*

Do It Now!

'Ruth said do it now. Do it! It wasn't the first time but I was still unsure about kicking him out so rudely. After all, I quite liked him.'

The above sentence, used as inspiration, resulted in the following stories which range from ghostly encounters, emotional distress, an inexperienced trainee, to problematic pets.

EPISODES Flash Fiction - *by Cornflower Rose*

Ruth said it should happen now. Do it! It wasn't the first time, but I was still unsure of kicking him out so rudely. After all, I quite liked him.

His behaviour is sometimes very unnerving, but he's harmless. You can tell when he is having one of his 'episodes' as he talks incessantly about god and religion. It's usually a sign that he isn't taking his medication.

Ruth feels intimidated by him, but I know if you just humour him, he'll calm down and not do anything rash. He can be quite funny really and, once you realise this, there isn't a problem. Kicking him out won't help as he'll wander off in a terrible state of mind. Then who knows what he'll do?

TOUGH LOVE *by Jasmine Rose*

Ruth said, "It should happen now. Do it." It wasn't the first time but I was still unsure of kicking him out so rudely. After all, I quite liked him.

This relationship was unlike any I had been involved in before, it wasn't easy and I was seriously beginning to think I had made a mistake. After all, this is my home, my refuge, my haven. It felt like he had invaded my space, I was on edge, I had to keep my eye on him all the time. How could everything go so wrong so quickly?

I was drawn to him from the first moment I saw him. He attracted me to him in a way that none of the others had done. His quirkiness appealed to me and I was certain that he was the one who could bring me the companionship I needed. I didn't want to lose him.

Ruth knew I had made the right decision and I know I can trust her in matters like this - she has so much more experience than me. She knows how to handle them! "He doesn't know he is doing anything wrong, you need to be firm with him. He is very young. What does he know about pristine, unblemished carpets, how much they cost! How hard you worked to get them! When he wants to pee, he pees! That's what dogs do."

I know she is right, heartless as it seems (it is so cold outside and he is so cute and cuddly). I know he is good for me and I am very, very fond of him but, if he and I are going to live together, I need to toughen up. I won't kick him out, but from now on, when he pees on the carpet - out he goes!

IN TRAINING *by Lavender Rose*

(Suitable to be read with slightly older children)

Ruth said, "It should happen now." It wasn't the first time but I was still unsure of kicking him out so rudely. After all, I quite liked him. He had potential.

But the rules are clear: detect, respect, collect and payment protect and he had undoubtedly broken every single one.

Maybe he does need to go back. With further training maybe, just maybe, further disaster can be averted.

Detection can be quite tricky for a trainee. Youngsters put their teeth under the pillow and dream of rewards NOT rude awakenings. After poking noses, knocking things over and tickling necks, no-one spotted his twinkling eyes and cheeky grin, sleep was disturbed and they just wailed. As always Ruth said he had to be stopped. "It should happen now. He'll have to go, he just can't stay, back to school is the only way."

But I was still unsure of kicking him out so rudely. I quite liked him, he had potential.

What a shame his second night on duty was Halloween. He showed no respect wearing that scary monster costume. It completely hid his twinkling eyes and cheeky grin. All his clumsiness awoke the youngsters and when they saw the monster they were so frightened.

Ruth had seen enough. "He'll have to go, he just can't stay, back to school is the only way."

But I was still unsure of kicking him out so rudely. I quite liked him, he had potential.

Night three was a little better. Only about half the youngsters he visited were woken up, and his gentle singing meant they drifted quickly back to happy dreams and remembered nothing. But he snagged his collection bag on a window sill and lost every single tooth. He had failed to collect.

"Disaster," said Ruth. "No more chances. He'll have to go, he just can't stay, back to school is the only way."

But I was still unsure of kicking him out so rudely. I quite liked him, he had potential.

And he pleaded and pleaded for one last chance and with those twinkling eyes and cheeky grin how could we resist.

Last night, was the worst of all. Payment protect went out the window. Young ants were given pennies that nearly squashed them and their grown-ups thought there had been an earthquake.

Puppies were given leaves that tickled their noses and made them sneeze and their grown-ups were worried that they were catching a cold.

Children were given bones and their grown-ups were not happy to find these disgusting, smelly objects under their children's pillows, and would not listen to their protests, "I didn't do it! But… can we get a puppy?"

There were too many mistakes. "THAT IS IT!" said Ruth. "Enough! He'll have to go, he just can't stay, back to school is the only way!"

But I was still unsure of kicking him out so rudely. I quite liked him, he had potential.

"Nice as he is and no matter how much you like him, he's hapless, he's hopeless, it should happen now," said Ruth. "He'll have to go, he just can't stay, back to school is the only way."

Maybe Ruth is right, he'll have to go back. Hopefully he's a fast learner and with his twinkling eyes and his cheeky grin he'll soon learn and be back with us again.

SID *by Red Rose*

Ruth said it should happen now, do it! I know it wasn't the first time he had misbehaved, but I was still unsure of kicking him out so rudely. After all, I quite liked him.

That first week when he made himself known, I couldn't see him, I just started finding things out of place and at the same time every night a strong smell of tobacco would fill the air. It unnerved me at first but totally freaked my sister Ruth out.

As time went on he made himself more apparent and friends gradually stopped popping round, visitors were almost non-existent. Ruth warned me, "They're scared you know, and you can't blame them, they just don't know what'll happen next, the flickering lights, the footsteps on the stairs…"

"He's not malicious, just a bit mischievous," I found myself defending him to Ruth. I'd even given him a name, I called him Sid! Plucked it out of thin air like, don't know where it came from.

"Oh, and what about Alan?" she said, her voice rising an octave. "Look what happened there then." Alan was my ex-boyfriend. He put up with the odd goings on in a fashion, but when the TV kept turning off during the football, he spat his dummy out, and that was the last I saw of him. No great loss really.

Ruth had taken it upon herself to ring a psychic, who volunteered to come around to the house, to see if she could tell us anything about what was happening and why. To be honest I went along with this just to shut her up.

Anyway, up turns Gloria, a nice lady. She sensed him straight away, although he was very quiet. I think he knew why she was there.

Her eyes glazed over and she started to talk, "He's attached to this house and doesn't want to leave, there's no harm in him he just likes to be acknowledged. Oh, but he didn't like your boyfriend love," she said, raising her eyebrows at me.

I sighed, "I know, I think he was a good judge of character to be honest!"

Ruth rolled her eyes, "Give me strength!"

Gloria passed me her card. "If you want me to send him to the light love, here are my details, just get back in touch."

After she left I felt quite sad. Of course Ruth was up for it. "Just get rid of the old git once and for all," she voiced most unsympathetically. But I was still unsure. After all I was used to Sid, he was company in an odd sort of way, and the house never felt empty.

He was quiet that night, and the night after that. On the third night, I poured myself a glass of wine and curled up on the sofa.

"Sid, are you still here?" Five minutes later the smell of his tobacco wafted in front of me and I smiled. After all, I quite liked him!

Chapter Eight

"Of new acquaintances one can never be sure because one likes them one day that it will be so the next. Of old friends one is sure that it will be the same yesterday, today and forever"

George Eliot

Lucy Drummond

It's amazing how a line dropped into an innocent conversation, ***"Her name is Lucy Drummond and we're meeting her at twelve,"*** can suggest different concepts such as misheard words, feelings of insecurity and life-long ambitions.

THE BABYSITTER *by Cornflower Rose*

Slamming the front door as he left the house, a very disgruntled Kian marched down the road. At ten years of age he thought he knew everything. Why he was practically grown up! What did he need a babysitter for? Ok, yes occasionally he had to be reminded to pick up his toys scattered all over his bedroom floor. Oh, and just occasionally to brush his teeth, and wash his face and hands. Maybe he played too much on his Playstation and watched too much telly, but did that mean he had to have a babysitter? He could make himself a drink and a sandwich, he didn't need anyone to show him how to do that! Most of the time he remembered to turn lights off, not to cross the road unless he stopped, looked right, left and right again and listened for traffic. He could ride his bike without stabilisers, but only sometimes needed reminding to wear his helmet. That wasn't a hanging offence, was it? Nah! Resolutely he'd decided he would put his foot down and downright refuse to have a stranger babysit him!

When Mum had told him that her best friend's niece was coming for a couple of hours that afternoon, so that they could get to know each other before she started babysitting, he'd had a bit of a tantrum. He'd stamped his feet and shouted, "No I don't need a babysitter, I'm not a baby," and promptly threw his bowl on the floor, scattering cereal everywhere.

"Kian! You will clean that mess up right now, that's certainly the behaviour of a baby!" Mum shouted, "and another thing, you know Grandma's not very well, so you are getting a sitter and I don't want to hear another word about it. Her name is Lucy Drummond and we're meeting her at twelve."

Furious, Kian grabbed a pan and brush and began his clean-up operation, but not before giving his mother a look that would stop a clock.

Storming down the road, in a fit of pique, he wondered if he should call for his best friend Jack, who lived in the next street. Jack was out shopping with his Mum, so he tried Millie, but she was horse riding and Reece was not at home either. Feeling a bit sorry for himself he took himself off to the playground around the corner. The weather wasn't too bad, a bit overcast and dull but warm for October. Being a school holiday, the park was quite busy so he had to wait to get a turn on the swings. The girl on the next swing was older, about 15 or 16 and dressed funny, or so he thought. Her clothes were all black and she wore big chunky boots with zips and studs all over them and bright green laces. On her face she had thick make-up, thick black eye-liner and black lipstick. Her hair was black also and cropped short, sticking up all over and she had studs in her nose and ears. Looking closely at her he said,

"Do those hurt?"

"Does what hurt?" she replied.

"Those things on your nose and ears. They look funny."

"Never feel them, they don't bother me," she said. "What's your name shorty?"

"Kian, what's yours?"

"I like to be called Jet. All my mates call me that."

Muttering under his breath, he said, "That's a weird name!" They struck up a conversation and Kian grumbled and moaned and told Jet about being unhappy about getting a sitter. Jet listened and said it was tough, but there were some things, when you were ten, you can't do anything about. She said that you can't make judgements about people you don't know and maybe he should think on, that his Mum and Dad wouldn't ask someone to babysit their precious little boy if they were horrible or nasty, would they? Reluctantly, Kian had to agree. He quite enjoyed talking to Jet and followed her round the park for a while and they chatted about everything under the sun. She was nice and she was right as well - you shouldn't judge people. Jet looked very different but was kind and pleasant.

At home, as 12 o'clock drew near, Kian got butterflies in his stomach. What if the sitter made him stay in his room all afternoon? With trepidation, he looked out of his bedroom window to catch a glance of the dreaded sitter. What if she was really horrible after all? Imagine his surprise when the mystery figure approached the front door. His heart thumping in his chest, he sprang out of his room and took the stairs two at a time, to be there to open the door before his Mum,

"Hello Shorty, how you doing?" she laughed.

"Jet, it's you - are you my babysitter?"

"Yes I am and I think we are going to have some fun aren't we?"

"Oh! Yes," cried Kian, "I can't wait, I'm glad it's you."

Mum and Dad stood there with their mouths gaping open, who had kidnapped their child and replaced him with this pleasant, polite one? Wonders will never cease.

LIVING THE DREAM *by Jasmine Rose*

Horse racing was in his blood, always had been - for as long as he could remember. Ryan couldn't think of a time when he didn't want to spend every spare moment he had, cycling over to Jack Wilson's stables, just to be near the horses. He loved to watch the stable lads taking them through their paces and, if he was given the chance to help with the mucking out or bringing in the feed during the long, cold winters, he was in seventh heaven! Ryan soon found ways of making himself useful. He was a likeable lad and no one minded having him around.

His parents couldn't understand him. He was clever and they wanted him to pursue a more academic career. They saw good exam results, university and a steady career path as the way forward.

"Not for me," Ryan always retorted on those times when they succeeded in pinning him down to 'discuss his future.'

When he was sixteen he approached Mr Wilson and asked if he could be taken on as one of the stable team. Jack had no problem saying yes. He had watched Ryan with the horses and he recognised the lad's gift for communicating with them. He had an innate understanding of their characters and was quick to sense their moods. He knew how to handle them. It wasn't long before Ryan became affectionately known as the 'Wilson Whisperer!'

Jack was keen for Ryan to complete the Apprentice Learning Course. He approached the lad's parents in an effort to encourage them to support their son.

"The lad is a natural," he told them. "He was born to ride and has the potential to be a great jockey one day."

Jack was proud of him and pushed Ryan to complete the Apprentice Advance Course and it wasn't long before Ryan's name began to rise in the ranks of successful riders. As Jack had forecast, Ryan was good - very good, but that was not enough for Ryan, he wanted to be a champion jockey!

Again, it was Jack who helped him to take a further step forward towards achieving the success he longed for. Jack's friend, Robert Langton from a neighbouring training stable, was a jockey short. His best rider had taken a nasty fall and would be out of action for the 1,000 Guineas at Newmarket. Jack recommended Ryan to him and told the lad to ring Mr Langton to arrange a visit.

"Did you manage to speak to Bob?" he asked Ryan when he saw him the following morning.

"Yes, I did." Ryan's eyes were shining with excitement. "He wants me to see his horse. Her name is Lucy Drummond and I'm meeting her at 12 o'clock."

"Good lad, I'll come with you."

That first meeting was the start of a legendary partnership between horse and jockey. She was skittish, unpredictable and fast! He was strong, persuasive and he knew how to ride a horse such as she.

The big day arrived and Ryan knew he was facing the biggest challenge of his career. It felt strange to be wearing the Langton colours but he had the confidence of knowing he had Jack's blessing. Lucy D, as she was affectionately known, was jumpy that day. She had a wild look in her eyes and Ryan remembered the difficulty he had in getting her into the starting gate. Fortunately, the blindfold had not been necessary but her tetchiness made him very uneasy.

"Don't worry L.D," he whispered in her ear. "We're together in this." His calming words did nothing to stop her bolting from the gate like a bullet out of a gun.

"Not so fast girl, not so fast." Ryan gently but firmly pulled on the reins and pressed his knees into her sides, struggling to stay in control. He knew they were in danger of being boxed in on the inside. L.D. had the speed but they needed to find a way through the field if they were to be in with a chance.

"Easy Lucy, easy," he said softly and his cajoling tone quietened and calmed the highly-strung filly. L.D. responded by holding back, searching for the way forward.

A narrow gap opened before them, the grey to their left and a robust chestnut to the right. He felt L.D.'s stride lengthen as she slipped through the gap, easing her way towards the front of the field, gathering speed as the way ahead opened up before them. The wind whistled past Ryan's ears, only two horses before them now and the finish line in view! Could they do it? L.D.'s ears flattened against her head and her stride lengthened even further as the crowd roared them on. They were flying! The gap was closing, and he could hear the laboured breathing and the pounding of the hooves of their competitors. The sound of the riders' whips lashing through the air as they urged their horses on told Ryan all he needed to know. They were through! The crescendo of sound surrounded them as they crossed the line a full length ahead of their nearest rival.

'LUCY DRUMMOND, RIDDEN BY RYAN WAITES AND TRAINED BY ROBERT LANGTON, HAS WON THE 1,000 GUINEAS!'

Those words were among the sweetest Ryan had heard during the course of his career. Whenever he closed his eyes he could transport himself back in time to the sweetness and thrill of that moment. Many triumphs had followed and Ryan had now reached the greatness he had yearned for in the hierarchy of the racing world. He had worked hard and sacrificed much, but he knew he could never have achieved the status he now enjoyed without the support of his mentor Jack Wilson and the supreme magnificence of his equine superior, the truly amazing Lucy Drummond.

SEA-DRUM *by Lavender Rose*
(Suitable to be read with younger children)

Mum had been talking, but Alex had not been listening. He had been thinking about putting on the pink tutu and riding on the red scooter. He wished he had been listening because he thought Mum had said that Grandad Lou had a sea-drum and… that sounded interesting. Alex had a plastic drum made of plastic and nursery had a wooden drum made of wood with calfskin on top. But a sea-drum couldn't be made from sea because it would be splashy and flow away when you banged it.

Liam had got the tutu first and Mona was riding on the red scooter first. Alex decided to ask his nursery friends to find out exactly what a sea-drum is.

So, he asked Ava who was always playing on the slide, going down as fast as she could. She said, 'if it's not made of sea, maybe… it was made by the sea?'

Then he asked Bertie who was playing with the wooden blocks making a bear cave. He said, "if it's not made of sea, maybe… sea fishermen on their boats bang it to catch more fish?"

Then he asked Cora who was playing in the kitchen making cakes. She said, "if it's not made of sea, maybe… you drop sea water on it instead of playing it with sticks or hands?"

Then he asked Digby who was digging in the mud making a deep hole. He said, "if it's not made of sea, maybe… it tells sea ships which way to go so they don't get lost?"

Then he asked Ella who was drawing an enormous emerald elephant. She said, "if it's not made of sea, maybe… sea water is used to make it sound better if it stops working?"

Then he asked Freddie who was putting together a farm animal jigsaw. He said, "if it's not made of sea, maybe… it makes sharks dance in the sea and not try to eat people?"

Then he asked Gail who was putting shells around the sand garden she'd made. She said, "if it's not made of sea, maybe… mermaids play it and the sea shell creatures come to play with them?"

Then he asked Henri who was reading a story to his teddy about a mouse house. He said, "if it's not made of sea, maybe… it sounds like the sea hitting the beach when it's played?"

Then he asked Ida who had washed all the dressing up clothes and was going to iron them. She said, "if it's not made of sea, maybe… it's a seal drum made with seal skin?"

Then he asked Jordan who was listening to a story about a jumping jaguar on the interactive board. He said, "if it's not made of sea, maybe… dolphins sing along to it in the sea?"

Then he asked Kira who was kicking balls to a toy kangaroo. She said, "if it's not made of sea, maybe… you can win them at the shows on the sea-side pier?"

Then mum arrived. "We need to be quick," she said. "We need to get back before Lucy."

Alex wanted to know who Lucy was. "My friend from when I was a little girl," said Mum. "I told you on the way to nursery this morning. She's called Lu_CY_ _DRUM_m_ond_ and she wants to meet us as at 12."

"Oh," said Alex, "I thought you said Grandad Lou's _sea-drum_ _and_…?"

He still wondered what a sea-drum was, but maybe... Lucy Drummond might know.

<u>To think about...</u>

What mistake did Alex make?

What are your favourite toys at places you visit?

What materials have any drums you have seen been made of?

Ask a grown-up to help you make a drum to play.

Will you sing or dance when you play your drum?

What do you notice about Alex's friend's names?

What might his other friends be called?

What do you think they might have said a sea drum is?

FEELING BLUE *by Red Rose*

It was their second meeting. Jill sat there with her arms folded defensively across her stomach, as Lucy got them both a drink from the water cooler. Jill stared at the machine mesmerized by the colour of it, a beautiful calming blue and her favourite colour. Shuffling in her seat she shifted her gaze to the clock on the wall, it was 12 o'clock. She hoped the hour session would pass quickly.

Placing the water carefully on the desk, Lucy sat down with a smile, clipped the name badge, **Lucy Drummond - Therapist** to her blouse then turned her chair towards her client.

"How are you today Jill?"

Jill took a sip of water and thought about her answer, "Ok... I think. I didn't sleep too well, but that's nothing new. I'm used to it now."

Lucy glanced down at her notes, "Ahh yes, we touched on this last week didn't we. So, have any of the suggestions we talked about helped in any way?"

"No, not really." If truth be told the only thing Jill had done differently was spray some Lavender Sleep Spray on her pillow, but she wasn't going to tell Lucy that.

Lucy rummaged through the papers on her desk and passed Jill another copy of the

20 Tips to Help You Get a Good Night's Sleep - information sheet.

Jill rolled her eyes, it should be renamed - 'Rid Yourself of the Only Pleasures in Life' information sheet! But she kept that thought to herself.

Lucy smiled encouragingly, "Well let's give it another week. How are things at home, with Colin?"

Jill fidgeted nervously, wringing her hands. "He's not very supportive to be honest, he feels embarrassed about what happened, he can't believe what I did and feels I've humiliated him." She smirked a little as she pictured Colin's incredulous face as he arrived to pick her up from the police station.

The rest of the hour was spent talking about her relationship with pillar of the community Colin, and the way this wretched menopause was affecting them. The night sweats, the brain fog and the Jekyll and Hyde mood swings. It was hell.

The anxiety was horrendous. It had taken its toll on Colin when she became rooted to the spot at the bottom of the stairs in the shopping centre. They were open backed and there was no way she could have walked up them, her fear of falling was too great.

He doesn't understand how she feels, how could he? Yes, of course she feels guilty about taking that blue pair of lady's luxury socks and being banned from the store for 6 months - along with a police caution and a fine. That's part of what keeps her awake at night.

All he does is prattle on about unimportant things. It was the last straw when he grumbled he wanted scrambled eggs instead of poached. I'll give him scrambled she thought and came this close to crowning him in the kitchen with the poaching pan.

"Where is all this anger coming from?" She asked Lucy, "I used to pander to his every whim. Am I going insane or have I seen the light?"

Lucy listened attentively making all the right noises in all the right places whilst scribbling the odd note.

Her doctor wouldn't prescribe HRT, he said she was too young at forty-three even though she was going through an early menopause. So, with her HRT hopes dashed she decided to go down the homeopathic route.

The lady in the health food shop was very knowledgeable. She patted her on the arm and said it was quite common. She had a number of menopausal women coming in with urges to bray their husbands, and pointed her in the direction of the Red Clover tablets.

Lucy glanced up at the clock as the session was drawing to an end. "Ok Jill, the tablets may take a few weeks to start working, so give them a chance and keep trying the sleep techniques. I'll see you in a week's time."

As Jill set off on her walk through the shopping centre to get back to her car, the heat started sweeping over her, Oh no... not again! In a panic, she searched in her bag for her faithful friend, the battery-operated fan that was her constant companion these days. It gave little relief as the perspiration ran down the back of her neck and droplets formed on her forehead.

It was unbearable, was she going to spontaneously combust? Standing in a shop doorway she waited for the hot flush to pass. Glancing up she caught a glimpse of herself in the mirror placed in the window display. What a sight! She saw the jowly face, sunken eyes, and haggard expression looking back at her and realised she was losing herself. The void she felt inside was gnawing away at her and getting bigger, until she spotted the jumper, in a pile, all nicely folded. It was a beautiful calming blue, that very same blue of the water cooler that stood in Lucy Drummond's room. The adrenaline was pumping as she entered the store and picked it up, walking behind a rail of clothes as she stuffed it into her bag. The fix, albeit brief, was satisfying.

Chapter Nine

"Autumn is a second spring when every leaf is a flower"

Albert Camus

Burgundy Boots

'*Wearing her burgundy boots, she was happily kicking the autumn leaves, when...*'

A simple pleasure like kicking through the autumn leaves - giving a person time to contemplate on times gone by, surreal experiences and life changing outcomes. What adventures could lie ahead, is there something sinister beneath the leaves?

Thank you, Black Rose for your contribution to this chapter.

THE LITTLE BOX *by Cornflower Rose*

She was happily kicking the autumn leaves, transfixed in a world of her own thoughts. The colours all around adding to the surreal ambience; reds, browns, golds, and greens cascading to the ground on to the lush forest carpet beneath her burgundy booted feet. The leaves crisp, cracking and crunching. The air cool and sharp, the sky blue and wintery. Not another soul around. The only sounds heard were her footsteps and the inhaling and exhaling of her breath as she ambled along.

Shuffling her feet as she walked, Paula's thoughts were all in a quandary. She was remembering her best friend Molly, who had sadly passed away two years ago. She felt the pain of grief, whenever she remembered Molly, especially as she was still relatively young when she passed. They had become very close in their twenties when they had ventured into business together, setting up and running a successful pottery shop in their home town. It was a hectic time, combining rearing of young children and working hard to establish themselves in a competitive market. But they thoroughly enjoyed every moment of it.

Poignantly, she thought of the weekend away they had awarded themselves to celebrate their success. Feeling liberated they'd booked a long weekend to London, going to a West End show, shopping and sight-seeing. They'd had a great time, and on the last afternoon, before heading home, they'd found themselves in Covent Garden, browsing around the trendy, artisan craft stalls at the indoor market place. Molly bought two matching little jewellery boxes, each had beautiful mother of pearl inlay on the lids and little silver keys. Giving one to Paula, she'd said it was to always remind her of their great time in London. It was ideal for holding treasured little keepsakes.

Feeling a stab of guilt she remembered hers was now sat in the back of a dressing table drawer, full of odd buttons, pins, and a plethora of useless items. She hadn't looked at it for a long time. She just knew that it was there. Molly's box was also in the drawer. When she'd died her partner had said that Molly had left a request to pass the box on to Paula, as it probably meant more to her than to him. She'd been delighted to get it. But what she found in that little box had changed her life. She remembered now how she'd taken the box and gone into her bedroom to spend a few moments in contemplation, and to see what pieces of treasure Molly had kept.

Gingerly she had unlocked the box with the little key. She saw that it held some costume jewellery; ear rings, brooches and a thin silver chain with a silver locket - inside a photo of them both, taken in their carefree days. Paula remembered giving it to Molly for her fortieth birthday, she'd laughed and said she loved it. Tears stinging her eyes, she remembered removing the jewellery. The bottom of the box was covered with a scrap of red velvet material. She could see that it was loose and when she lifted it, she had noticed folded paper lining the bottom. It had been folded small enough that it could not be seen until the jewellery had been removed.

When she'd taken it out and carefully unfolded it, she was surprised to see copies of birth and adoption certificates. Not understanding what she was looking at - she'd sat on the end of her bed, and scrutinised the details, not believing what she was reading. It showed the mother of a baby boy born on 26th January 1985, was Molly and that the boy named Robert had been adopted a week later. Working out the dates it meant Molly was only fifteen at the time of his birth. What a revelation! Molly had never uttered a word of this in all their years of friendship. Paula's heart was breaking for Molly, thinking of how she must have yearned all these years for the boy she'd given away and having to lock the secret deep inside never to reveal it to a soul.

Surely receiving the box under Molly's express wishes could only mean one thing. Paula wanted to find Molly's boy and let him know what a wonderful person Molly had been.

Using every genre of social media available she had set out on a quest. It was painstaking and at times disappointing, hitting red tape and other brick walls. But her arduous quest had eventually paid off through the power of Facebook. She had finally located Robert.

They were going to arrange a meeting soon, and she was feeling nervous, apprehensive and worried. What was she going to tell the young man who had been given away so soon after he was born?

She just prayed that Molly would be pleased with her efforts. She had been busy writing a journal from memory about Molly and her achievements, and hoped that Robert would love the essence of Molly. She wanted him to appreciate what a wonderful person she had been and that he could be proud to say she had been his birth mother. That was Paula's deepest wish.

A DIFFERENT HORIZON *by Jasmine Rose*

Lizzie was happily kicking the autumn leaves which generously carpeted the ground beneath her feet. This was her favourite place to enjoy being outdoors. She loved the solitude of the woods which bordered the walkway near her parents' house. She was content to stroll, thankful for this brief period of time to feel at peace with herself, a short hiatus in which she could catch her breath before taking the next step in her life's journey.

She knew she was on the brink of making one of the biggest decisions of her life and she had worked her socks off to bring herself to this point. Lizzie wanted to be sure she had thought her decision through, the pros and the cons, before she finally made it.

Her phone rang, jolting her back into current awareness. As she glanced at the screen, she saw that it was Rob. "Hi, any news yet?" he asked.

"Not yet," Lizzie replied, "it looks as though it will be tomorrow before the results are on the notice board." It irritated her that he rang each day because she had told him she would let him know as soon as she knew how she had done. She felt guilty because he irritated her - he didn't deserve that.

"I'll ring you tomorrow Rob. Em and I are meeting early at Uni. We want to be sure we are there before the results are made public."

Lizzie looked down at the leaves and marvelled at how vibrant they were, they gave pleasure even when they were dying! The sight of them caused her to reflect yet again on the cycle of life. The leaves had lived their lives to their full purpose and Lizzie knew this thought lay at the root of her problem - she didn't feel that she was living her life to the full. She wanted more; she longed to travel and explore the world. 'Reach for the moon, if you miss you will still be among the stars.' She remembered those words spoken by a friend when she had voiced her intention of applying for a place at university. Lizzie wanted a future in which she could tell her children stories about her adventures. She wanted to look into their wide eyes and relive the excitement and wonderment of her travels.

"You always were fanciful," her mother would say with a scornful tone whenever Lizzie transported herself into the world of make believe and fairy stories. Lizzie thought her mother's imagination must have been left in the womb on the day she was born.

"Stay with what you know and be grateful for what you have." Her mother's mantra relayed itself over and over again in her mind.

Lizzie was grateful for what she had. She appreciated everything her Mum had done for her, but surely that didn't mean she couldn't want more? She had tried very hard to live down to her mother's expectations of her. She had left school at sixteen and secured a steady job (with good prospects) in local government. Rob was a good friend and Lizzie knew she would have a safe and secure life with him, but he seemed to be governed by the same lack of imagination and adventure as her mother. She would suffocate!

They had both looked at her as if she had completely lost her senses when she told them she had enrolled at Leeds University to study Politics and Comparative Studies.

"University! Politics! Comparative Studies!" they spluttered. "What on earth for?" Lizzie didn't try to explain, what was the point?

She had lived in the halls during her first year as an undergraduate and had met Emily during Fresher's Week. They had gravitated towards each other and now Lizzie felt Emily was the best friend she had ever had.

Em was a single parent, something her parents found it difficult to forgive her for. She had worked as a nursery assistant and managed to raise her son, Ben, without being too dependent on others. Her mother had thawed a little when Emily enrolled as an undergraduate and she offered to help look after Ben whenever she was needed. Money was always short and Em's Christmas and birthday presents always took the form of Marks and Spencer vouchers.

Lizzie knew her friend would rather have cash. She remembered the look on Em's face when they had seen the boots in Hatters window. She thought it was a strange name for a shoe shop, but agreed with Em that the boots were beautiful. A gorgeous burgundy red, boots to add a touch of chic to any outfit, no matter how hardwearing and sensible it was!

The coloured leaves at her feet brought back the memory of Emily's look of longing. It still surprised Lizzie that they had come from such different backgrounds but their friendship never wavered. They were both ambitious, but for different things. How proud they had been when they graduated, Lizzie with an upper second class degree and Emily with a first!

When the TESOL post graduate course was offered, both of them jumped at the opportunity. For Lizzie, teaching English as a second language to overseas learners, was a ticket to work her way round the world! For Emily, it offered an opening for work in education, a chance to plan a structured career - a safe future for Ben. Their teaching placements at the International Centre opened their eyes to the diversity of cultures and languages to be explored.

Lizzie sighed as she brought her thoughts back to the present. She had broached the subject of travel with her Mum and Dad but they had accused her of being fanciful and irresponsible again.

"Will you never grow up!" her mum had retorted.

"What about Rob?" Her dad had responded in a more studied tone.

It worried her that Rob would be hurt when she went away, but she knew she would hurt him more if she stayed. She was resolute about her decision.

The two friends met in the uni refectory next morning. Emily was full of excitement at the prospect of two interviews, one of which was for a permanent teaching post at the International Centre.

"My black suit will have to do because I certainly can't afford anything new at the moment. My old boots will polish up well and maybe I can treat myself to a new scarf."

"You will look fantastic and they will be stupid if they don't choose you," Lizzie responded, giving her friend a warm hug. When they heard shuffling and murmuring behind them they realised the results of the examinations were being pinned to the notice board. Taking a deep breath they manoeuvred their way to the front of the group crowding around the board, anxiously looking for their own names.

"Well done Lizzie!" Emily beamed and threw her arms around her friend's neck.

"Well done you Em. Haven't we done well?" Indeed they had, both credited with Grade A's.

Congratulations and cheers were shared with their other friends and they all arranged to meet that evening for a proper celebration. Lizzie arranged to call at Emily's house and they would come back into town together. Before going home, she popped into the shopping centre.

When her friend opened the door that evening, Lizzie placed a big box tied with a beautiful deep red bow into her hands. Emily's eyes nearly popped out of her head when she opened it.

"Knock 'em dead," Lizzie chuckled, as Em gazed at the beautiful burgundy boots.

Six months later, Lizzie was still filled with the joy and elation of that day. Here she was, living in Paris, teaching English to students who shared the same dreams as she had when she was a student! It had been a massive leap of faith but she had been given good advice and made really helpful contacts through her tutors at university.

She loved Paris, especially on days like today. She had strolled down the Champs-Élysée**s** and was now enjoying coffee and croissants at her favourite cafe in the Tuileries.

"What do you think then?" she asked the person sitting next to her. She didn't really need words for a response. The look on her Mum's face told her all she needed to know - a look of wide eyed wonder!

"Do you think Dad will visit with you next time?"

"He most certainly will, I'll make sure of that." Lizzie liked to hear the note of assertiveness in her mother's voice.

MUCK NOT LUCK! *by Lavender Rose*
(suitable to be read with younger children)

Sara was enjoying the crunching sounds as she stamped and kicked the autumn leaves with her burgundy boots. She gave one enormous kick and up flew a huge brown, stinking, disgusting ball of slime. The brown slime flew through the air and landed 'slop,' on her mum's right hand as she was steering the buggy.

"Urg!" cried Mum in disgust and shook her hand. The brown, stinking slime landed 'blop,' on the door handle of a passing blue car.

When the lady in the passenger seat got out, the brown, stinking slime landed 'plop,' on to the back of a passing cat.

The offended cat jumped onto the car park wall and shook off the stinking brown slime, which landed 'slop,' on to the back wheel of a passing mobility scooter.

The rider smelled the disgusting stench of the brown stinking slime. She noticed a clean looking puddle nearby. First she drove through it, next she drove the back wheel through the grass on the verge. She then repeated the clean puddle and verge pattern for a second time, a third time and a fourth time, but she still went home and sprayed the wheels and the bottom of the scooter and her shoes four times with disinfectant, just for good measure to ensure that the stink and stench and germs were all gone.

The cat owner smelt the disgusting odour as soon as her pet entered though the cat flap. First, she cleaned the area with baby wipes, then washed her feline pet in the bath - three times just for good measure to ensure that the stink and stench and germs were all gone.

The car driver took the car through the car wash when he heard about the disgusting mess on the side of his car. Then he took it through again just for good measure, to ensure that the stink and stench and germs were all gone.

When they got home, Sara had to remove her own shoes as Mum's hand was so disgusting. Mum washed her hands and thoroughly cleaned the pram handle and cover and wheels (just incase).

"I'm glad Baby Bobby is asleep," said Mum. "I'll get him out after we've washed our hands and had a nice, warm shower and put on our fresh, clean clothes."

Later that day Harv and Dan were sharing sweets as they walked home from school. The paper bag split and their foam bananas landed on the recently dried pavement by the side of the grass verge. "Five second rule," said Harv.

"No!" said Dan. "We need to leave them. My Mam says you don't eat things that drop on the floor cos they could have bad germs on them."

Harv picked up a handful of foam bananas and ate them anyway.

Next morning on the way to school Harv started to feel poorly, he went very white, then was sick into a big pile of leaves.

Sara was enjoying the crunching sounds as she stamped and kicked the autumn leaves with her recently cleaned burgundy boots. She gave one enormous kick…

Keep kicking and enjoying the autumn leaves, but be sure you know what to do if you get something nasty on your boot or shoe!

To think about...

What colours do the leaves go in autumn?

What can you make with autumn leaves you find?

What should dog owners do when their dog does a poo?

What should you do if things drop on the floor?

What should you do if you get something nasty on your shoe?

Rambling Rose Writers

GRETCHENS GIFT *by Red Rose*

It was a crisp, cold day with glimpses of sunshine peeking through the clouds. Gretchen was in her favourite place, Elnath Park. Looking down at her feet, she admired the contrast of her patent leather burgundy boots against the rich golden hues of the leaves, crunching underfoot as they hid her path. With a smile as wide as the sea, she happily kicked them up in the air and they billowed, rustling around her legs as she walked, carefree and content without any warning of what was about to occur.

Suddenly her legs buckled as the ground beneath her seemed to suck her in. One gulp and she was enveloped up to her waist, her body stiffened as she let out a shriek. "Aaaahhh ... what's going on?" Her hands pushed down on the floor, trying to lift herself out, but all she could feel was the hard ground, gripping her vice like around the waist. "Help someone! Please help!" she sobbed, frantically looking around. But there was no-one about, it was eerily silent. Her breathing quickened, as everything she knew to be there, in her favourite place, seemed to swirl and move as if she was in a vortex.

Beneath her she felt a rumble coming up from the earth and the pulling started, "Noooo!" she screamed, as the rest of her body got sucked down through the leaves and pulled below with brute force. She held her breath as everything went black... surely she would suffocate. She landed with a jolt, that same feeling as when you're drifting off to sleep and you jump, waking yourself up, that kind of jolt. Her eyes were open but she couldn't see. Darkness surrounded her yet she was not afraid. Was she dead? She couldn't be, she could hear herself breathing.

As she tried to speak no words came out, only thoughts. 'Where am I?' Words that were not her own, in a voice that was neither male nor female came straight back at her, echoing around her head issuing instructions, "Look around."

Screwing up her eyes she thought, 'I can't see.'

"Do not use your eyes," the voice replied.

As she stared without seeing into the dark depths of the blackness surrounding her, she made her eyes relax and go out of focus, blurry like they used to when she looked at those magic eye books a few years ago. Gradually blue and white flashes of colour started to appear.

"Close your eyes," the voice commanded. She had the sensation of being wrapped up in a blanket and felt warm, comfortable and safe.

'Why am I here?' she implored.

The voice seemed to enter every pore of her being. "You have been given this gift Gretchen, the power to see into the future, the ability to enter a person's mind, heart and soul. You will see the outcome of their impending decisions and the consequences they could have, on humankind and planet earth. You will act on this. There are more of you, and in the course of time you will find each other and make a difference."

She was conscious of every molecule in her body moving and vibrating, her whole being seemed connected to a source of energy.

"Now open your eyes," she heard the voice above everything else. Her head was full of thoughts and ideas that were not her own, she had answers to things she knew nothing about.

"Look into the darkness," it said, and as she did she saw spots of gold floating in the distance, multiplying as they advanced towards her.

"Go back to the leaves now," and as she thought about the leaves, the spots in front of her started to swirl.

"More," the voice boomed. As she pictured them in her mind - beautiful, crisp, autumnal and golden - a huge circle of swirling leaves enveloped her like a cocoon, picking her up and thrusting her back up through the earth and placing her gently on the ground, legs in front of her. Her burgundy boots shone as they peeped out from beneath the leaves.

She was back in her favourite place but everything seemed strange, she was different. Standing up, her legs trembling like a new born lamb, her senses heightened, she looked around in awe. She was aware of her advanced perception of the world, but unaware of the dilemmas she would have to face and the turmoil that lay ahead…

THE PIT *flash fiction by Black Rose*

She was happily kicking the autumn leaves when her life changed forever. Autumn turned to winter. Good to bad. Present to future. Nothing would ever be the same again. As a child she had read Alice in Wonderland. As Alice fell into the rabbit hole so did she. Unlike Alice she was never a child again.

Her first moments in the pit were little different to the years that followed. She wondered at first whether she was dreaming. She was not of course - as the leering half man, half goat sniggering at her in the corner was to remind her every day. She looked down at the burgundy boots that had so delighted her as she wore them straight from the shop that morning.

There in the pit it seemed like a different age, a different world. As her eyes grew gradually accustomed to the half-light she peered towards the beast, now manically giggling in the far corner. He perched on a neatly stacked pile of what she realised were bodies - many skeletal, some almost intact, all of them wearing burgundy boots.

Chapter Ten

"War is peace. Freedom is slavery. Ignorance is Strength"

George Orwell

-1984

War

What if…? People will always ponder the unknown. What would it be like if there was an alternative ending to World War 2? Here we have a futuristic view point, a sorry tale of oppression, celestial powers pulling the strings and poignant words written in rhyme.

THE LETTER *by Cornflower Rose*

She'd been longing for it to arrive for such a long time, and now that it was here, she was weak with anticipation. Maureen had been waiting for three months for a word from him, and now it had arrived she wasn't sure whether she could bear to read the contents.

Taking in a sharp breath, then releasing it slowly, she tore open the letter. Dated the 28th October 1950, Lamsdorf, Poland, she read:

My Darling Maureen,

I hope you received my last letter ok. I've re-read your last letter so many times that I think I have worn the print off.

Well, what can I say? The winter is now starting to settle in with a vengeance. It's hard to get warmed through. The meagre fire that we are allowed in our dormitory is hard to keep alight through lack of firewood, so we have devised a plan where we each take a turn to remove a board from our bunks to burn. It's not much but it helps a little. I'm writing this letter today, as you can see from the date, it's my birthday! 21 today. The guys tried to make it a bit special and memorable by making me a cake out of whatever ingredients they could find. To say it was memorable is an understatement. Still they meant well.

Nothing much has changed regarding our long and arduous work days. I never thought I would ever see myself as a miner, but that's the role that will be filling my days now, for how long I just don't know. The rumour mill has it that we must do 25 years as slave labourers. How can I endure it? 4 down and only 21 to go! It's exhausting and with the constant hunger it's so debilitating. Hunger is the worst thing (apart from missing you of course), they only supply us with enough food to keep us going. I long for fresh fruit and vegetables and proper bread. If you could see the horrible black stuff they have the nerve to call bread, you would cringe.

I count the days till my much longed for parcels arrive. Thank you by the way for the chocolate. I shared it with Harry and we had a veritable feast that day. I could really do with some new socks and gloves, if you could manage to acquire some. I've washed my socks so many times they are now thread-bare, thin and a bit holey. My boots are just about holding together, I just hope they last out till our next issue at Christmas.

Christmas, I am not looking forward to another one here in this place. Some of the guys in one of the other dormitories have managed to build a still and are producing alcohol, but I've heard that the results were not good, with reports of guys going temporarily blind and suffering severe diarrhoea. Think I'll give it a miss. I try to make my free time pass by playing cards, composing *letters to you and praying to the Lord for him to change the situation.*

I hope you and everyone at home (home - just writing the word is like a knife in my heart) are well and that you won't forget about me. Without your letters and parcels I don't know how I would carry on. Please write soon and let me know what's going on in your life - we hear nothing at all about what's going on in the world outside. Reading your letters keeps my spirits up over the long, cold months.

Take care of yourself and write soon,

All my love forever,

Jack

With tears in her eyes, Maureen sat down and contemplated how different things would have been if all the young able-bodied men had not been sent abroad to the continent as forced labour. Germany now ruling all of Europe and most of Africa, had changed their lives forever.

Looking back even the war years looked favourable - a carefree time. Now she had to work long hours in the steel works, doing a man's job. But she should be grateful, she could come home every night to food for the table and coal in the grate.

But it was a lonely existence without her Jack. Her life stretched before her as a single, childless woman and it was unbearable. Without the young men how was life to be created? No new generations to carry on the old traditions. How she hated Hitler and his Nazi followers, if only there had been a different outcome to the end of World War 2.

ALTERNATIVE EXISTENCE

by Jasmine Rose

Where now is our land of hope and glory?

So grey and unpleasant, a different story.

God did not save our gracious queen.

No rejoicing at her coronation.

Only a sombre acknowledgment of a king's collaboration.

"Heil Edward," some said.

As the crown of a turncoat was placed on his head.

No standing in streets with heads held high.

No smiling at neighbours under a clear blue sky.

Suspicion and fear soil the thoughts of the day.

Keep your tongue in your head, don't let it stray.

Colours of diversity, long since gone.

Their brightness obscured

By clouds of segregation and suffering endured.

It is hard to make progress and forge true tracks

With one eye glancing sideways

And the other looking back.

How bleak an outlook that would have been,

For a glorious land, so pleasant and green.

But righteousness conquered and England stayed free

To help the oppressed, wherever they may be.

And held fast the values which render the call

of Justice, Freedom and Equality for all.

Rambling Rose Writers

THE WORLD ANEW *by Lavender Rose*
(Suitable for older children)

ASSIGNMENT: Write a brief description of life on earth that could be read by a visitor from outer space to help them better understand our planet.

NAME: Julius Gywavbis

AGE: 12 years

It is 2045 and here on earth we are celebrating our centenary, 100 years of unity, peace and prosperity on earth.

This is a fantastic place to live. We are on a small planet that is spinning on an orbit around the sun.

All around us is sky. It looks amazing. In day time when we are facing the sun, it is light (even when you can't see the sun). The sky is constantly changing. There are clouds, rain, snow, wind, the sun and even the moon, all altering the way the sky looks. I love the oranges, yellows and reds of sunrises and sunsets. I like looking at the clouds where I can see amazing creatures, maybe they are the animals who used to live here? In the night time it is dark, but the moon reflects the light from the sun and at times gives light. The stars and planets can be seen from all around, looking different depending on where you are on earth.

The land itself can be so different depending on where you are. There are areas that are cold, with snow and ice all year round. Some places have vast areas of sand that changes with the wind. There are places with loads of plants and animals. In all these areas are seas and lakes and rivers and ponds. They are different too depending on the weather and the plants and animals that inhabit them. There are so many plants and animals living here on earth. We study and learn from them.

The plants grow and most use light and water and the goodness from the earth to produce oxygen, a gas that is good for keeping animals alive. Some live differently in water in streams and rivers and ponds and others live in the salty sea. There are tiny plants and huge trees. Some plants are pretty and others are plain, while others are ugly. Some are good to eat, others taste bad and smell disgusting, some cannot be eaten as they can cause illness and death. Many plants can only live in certain areas. Some can manage to live in areas above the clouds and obtain water to survive even though they get no rain.

The animals are even more amazing. Some are so tiny they can't be seen. Others are huge like whales and elephants. They eat plants for food, though some animals catch other animals as food and some need plants and animals in their diets. But they help each other as well and because of this all have better lives. I love watching the birds in spring, they prune and collect debris and clear and clean their local area as they make nest homes for their eggs.

Everywhere there are animals. They live on the land, in the water and in the sky. They move in different ways including, swimming, slithering, walking, running, climbing, flying. The smaller they are the more there tends to be. The larger animals tend to have smaller populations. Like the plants, some animals can only survive in certain areas on earth. To see them and how they live you have to be prepared to travel or you can watch and track them by electronic means in your living areas.

We are good custodians of The Earth. We make sure that the plants and animals live in harmony and each can thrive. We try to make sure every plant and animal has the best environment and enough food and water to survive.

We are able to understand many of the animals here. A big part of our education is studying the many languages of the earth's animals.

We are working to unify the language of each species. Previously each region had a different language. As animals are more able to travel and speak to their own species easily, we are working on developing a new common language so that each species can understand each other - this isn't so easy as we have to find sounds and actions each animal can make and perceive, then give them meaning.

We arrived here at a time when the earth's inhabitants were dysfunctional and distracted. They were in turmoil, intent on destroying each other in a war that involved everyone. It seems, in their futile fight for dominance, they failed to notice our arrival. We came in peace and tranquillity, but they were so entrenched in hatred and unrest that their life force fizzled and died out. We would have been happy to learn with them and try to gain a share in this beautiful place. Like the dinosaurs that once lived here, Homo sapiens became extinct, the earth beings, who seemed to be the highest life-form had perished. Behind them they left explosive devices – floating on balloons in the sky – hidden as land mines in the earth and in many types of weaponry – deteriorating and exploding in the water. Behind them they left animals captive and unhappy with tales of how they had been hunted and needlessly killed to satisfy superstition and greed.

We communicated with the life forms left and they were delighted for us to stay and share this glorious place with them.

What about us? We are over two-metres tall and our bodies glide easily over any terrain. We can change our body colour and smell to suit our mood. We choose from the colours in nature and aromas that surround us. The sunlight is our enrichment, it gives us our food and we need it to stay alive. We are much more efficient at using the sunlight than the plants and animals from here on earth, and we don't produce any by-products. This makes it far easier for us to travel through space than any of the lifeforms here.

So many adaptations have had to be made to provide food and water for earth animals on long journeys with us. We've had to incorporate new ways to dispose of their waste products - at one point there were fears they would pollute space with the amount of waste produced in a single year's journey. Fortunately, we were able to develop safe solutions.

Of course, we love to visit our planet of origin. Our biggest industries produce interplanetary transport and create interplanetary accommodation, entertainment and education.

Our travel programme is intense. We continue to explore and map the known and accessible universes. We hope to find life forms in other parts of the universe. Rest assured we hope we have learnt from our mistakes here. We will take every precaution to protect your safety. We look forward to working with you to enhance all our lives and will gladly share Earth and Ejcrbzhn with you.

We will show you how very different both of our planets are and how much we can learn from each other.

THE GRANDMASTERS' GAME (What If...)

by Red Rose

It was time for the next game. It had been brewing for a while. The Goddess Venusi normally serene, felt nervous. Jupe and Mercu the Gods, were pushing out their chests in anticipation of the battle.

She looked down through the clouds. It was her earth, she wanted to bathe it in peace. The Gods are Grandmasters, they desire war. She is saddened for what is about to happen, but knows there is no light without dark, no good without bad.

It is the experience of life for her humans, their lesson. This is how it's always been. As much as she longs to she cannot wrap them in cotton wool and shield them from what is to come. They are but pawns in these games of power.

"Now we shall start," thundered Mercu, his fists clenched.

Jupe squared up to him, "I am ready," he snarled.

Venusi moved in between them as the growling started deep within their beings.

Her cool, calm voice carried like the sound of the wind, "You are right, it is time." She led them over to the ornate gilt table and gestured them to sit.

"Let us drink," she passed them each a chalice of nectar infused with seeds of the poppy. It was a potent elixir she had mixed to diffuse their aggression.

There was no place for her at the table so she paced around it, seeking to soothe them with her peaceful presence.

The chess board was in the centre of the table. Venusi had seen to it they had chosen fairly. Mercu selected Germany and the Axis Powers, and then, by guessing the colour of the pawn in his opponent's hand he drew the white pieces, so he would move first.

Jupe drew Great Britain and the Allies. He was left with the black pieces. This would be a hard battle; she must try not to sway what the outcome will be.

Mercu with his white pieces moved first. Germany and the Axis powers quickly took control of the board. Venusi took a deep breath as she looked down on her earth, feeling the sadness of her humans as war was declared. She saw the bombs drop and her humans die.

Jupe was agitated as he looked down at the board. Venusi moved to his side and passed him the chalice. He drank and seemed calmer but was losing the battle; the game was getting nasty and nearing the end.

She could feel the pain and hear the screams coming up to her from the earth, her humans praying to their gods and goddesses for help. She could not answer their prayers yet.

Mercu unflinchingly took checkmate and bellowed, "I am the victor." He had taken Great Britain.

As Jupe howled in anger, Venusi gazed down at her earth, her tears landing on what had been her green and pleasant land. She saw the devastation happening in front of her eyes and could do nothing.

The game had ended. Mercu claimed victory, Germany had won.

Jupe slumped across the table, his groans making the earth shudder. He was wracked with grief and exhaustion. The game had lasted six earth years.

"Rest now," whispered Venusi, her voice caressing him. "You will play again soon, and for a different outcome."

Her head bowed she went back to look over her earth, her people, and the atrocities that war brings.

Her Japan, her Land of the Rising Sun, had dropped an atomic bomb on her Golden State, her California.

She viewed the destruction, the bleak and barren landscape below. More rain fell as her tears flowed. Much effort will be needed to tend her child.

She will give of her time to shower love upon her earth and her humans, to help them make the best of their plight and to learn their lesson.

She will call upon the sun to shine on the shadows, to help the flowers grow again and the birds to sing. She will do what she can with much love, until the next game...

Chapter Eleven

"The reason some portraits don't look true to life is that some people make no effort to resemble their pictures"

Salvador Dalí

Articles

Have you ever looked at an article or an advert in a magazine and conjured up a different scenario?

The writers, each in their own light-hearted style, penned a wonderful wacky poem, a budding romance, fear of scandal and hurt and loss.

From a suggestion by Fiona Veitch Smith - ***The Crafty Writers Creative Writing Course*** i.e. 'Use a cutting from a newspaper or magazine as a writing prompt.'

Special thanks to Margaret Dolan (Silver Rose) for her wonderful artistic representations of the articles we selected, preventing any breach of copyright.

HERBAL REMEDY
by Cornflower Rose

Cicely Montclair considered herself very lucky. She was sixty-nine years young and still relatively fit and healthy. She'd always kept herself trim by gardening - her true calling in life. She was fortunate that she had a decent sized garden where she could fulfil her passion.

In Middleton Wallop, she was known affectionately as, 'Cicely - The Herb Lady.' It made her laugh as she thought of the clever wag who had named her thus, her best friend Giles. He had a little allotment and used to take great pleasure in trying to outdo her efforts by cultivating his own herbs, but on a smaller scale. Good humouredly he tried to compete with Cicely but never managed to succeed. Secretly, he admired Cicely more than anyone he knew and if things had worked out differently - who knows? They may have married if he'd managed to pluck up the courage when he was younger, to propose to her. But that was water under the bridge as Cicely only had one great love in her life and that was her garden. She knew that Giles was in love with her and although she loved him as a friend, she had never felt the same way he did.

Every year both Cicely and Giles, in a light hearted competitive way, tried to cultivate an obscure herb and introduce it to the people of the village, in the hope they would use them in some fancy culinary dish. The local bistro, owned by a young trendy couple Dean and Dan, would accommodate their latest produce, by incorporating it into their popular pies, pastries, pasta and curry dishes. It worked well for both parties and the people of Middleton Wallop would decide which dish was the winner of the coveted, 'Herb of the Year Award,' presented by the local garden centre. Both Cicely and Giles kept it a close guarded secret which herb they were going to present.

Tonight, she was dressing very carefully for her visit to the Bistro with Giles. Always particular about her appearance, she took great care to apply her makeup. When satisfied she put on her favourite Jo Malone perfume, her subtle gold jewellery and with a final glance in the mirror declared herself ready.

Giles was waiting for her in her drawing room, with a small glass of sherry looking very pleased with himself. He was tall with a military bearing from his long service in the Army. He was always referred to as Sergeant Major, but in fact had gained the much higher rank of Brigadier. He had always tried to surprise Cicely with his choice of herb, but hadn't succeeded so far, as every year she seemed to pull some little-known species out of a hat and be announced the overall winner. This year he'd been determined to outclass Cicely and he thought he just might have done it. He couldn't wait to reveal his special find.

Cicely at the same time thought Giles was going to be blown away when she finally revealed her find. She just hoped Dean and Dan had managed to do it justice in one of their speciality dishes.

Seated now in the bistro, they were waiting with bated breath to see the menu and to try the prepared dishes. The bistro was full tonight, it usually was when they were having this tasting session. All their friends were just as keen to see who got to pick up the coveted award.

Two new dishes were added to the menu for tonight - a main dish of Chinese Special Curry and a dessert of Gooseberry Crème Brûlée Tart.

With great anticipation, they tucked into the Chinese food. Cicely knew that this was the one containing her secret herb. The food was delicious and she wondered if Giles would guess what it could be. He looked as if he too was relishing the food; she asked him if he knew what the secret ingredient was. Regretfully he shook his head and said he didn't have a clue. Cicely was delighted and couldn't wait to reveal it, but the pleasure must wait until the second dish was partaken.

Onto the dessert now, and both Giles and Cicely agreed that gooseberries were not their favourite of fruits, and given a choice, would normally not choose them. But in good spirits they ate it with gusto. Both were totally blown away with the tasty sweet dish. At last the time came for the clientele to choose their favourite of the two dishes and for the great reveal to be announced.

Over a glass of wine, they both waited apprehensively for the votes to be counted. At last Dean stood up and asked for silence whilst he read the results of the peoples vote.

"Ahh – erm, well folks, it would seem that for the first time ever we appear to have a draw. What shall we do now?" To a round of applause and pats on the back Cicely and Giles stood up. Being a gentleman Giles deferred to Cicely to go first to reveal her secret ingredient in the Chinese Curry Dish.

"Well, this year I searched long and hard to find something special that had meaning and was not very well known to the non-gardeners of the village. So, with my dearest friend Giles in mind I was absolutely ecstatic when I came across the little known Brigardiella, also known as the Giles Plant. An ideal addition to Chinese and Indian dishes. I'm sure you'll all agree it was a wonderful, spicy and tasty dish - just like Giles." Everyone laughed and agreed.

"Ha! Ha! Thank you my dear, I'm flattered. Now for my special herb this year, I also tried very hard to find something that would sum up the essence of Cicely. You are not going to believe me but the herb of my choice is called Sweet Cicely. It is ideal to use for sweetening sour dishes and just perfect to enhance sour tasting fruit like gooseberries."

Cicely and Giles stood transfixed, staring into each other's eyes in total disbelief. Ironically, they'd both had only the other in mind. It suddenly dawned on the pair of them that after all these years protesting they were both happy as they were, they realised that there was no other person they would rather share the rest of their life with.

So, by mutual agreement they decided to share the award. It would grace the mantelpiece in Cicely's cottage and when Giles moved in they would both be able to look at it every day and remember how they were finally brought together.

SPOKEN IN CONFIDENCE
by Jasmine Rose

"Do I have a head?" the marmot said.

"Of course you have," said Pete.

"If you stand up tall against a wall,

It's furthest away from your feet!"

PHYLLIS *by Lavender Rose*

She stared in shock at the paper. At least the photo wasn't on the front page. Even in her wildest dreams Phyllis had never imagined that if she appeared in the newspaper again, it would be in a picture of her in bed with an older man.

Phyllis bit at a nail as she began to ponder the implications. What would her family and friends think? Her poor husband! Might she be sued?

After she'd been made redundant life was hard. Although they'd taken out their mortgage at a good time, paying the bills and buying food was pushing them to the limit. They had never lived an extravagant life style. But they had been comfortable, managed a few treats like new clothes, keeping their home in good repair, nights out and a couple of value holidays most years.

She'd felt so guilty that soon she wouldn't be contributing to their income. After a year on job seekers allowance, her more than halved income had come to an end. She had tried so hard at job club, improving her computer skills and filling out endless application forms. She'd even had a few interviews, but they'd always chosen a younger candidate.

Their rainy-day savings were already gone. Knowing they were facing a further drop in income she'd strived even harder to save money. Shop value brands were now their staples. Her car had gone for scrap and now she walked everywhere or hitched a lift with friends and family. The exercise was beneficial and fortunately she was handy with a needle and thread to alter her old clothes to fit her less stocky figure.

Then she met Alf. She was swept off her feet by his charisma and sweet talk. She'd gone into their relationship with open eyes. But how had she been caught out in such a lie? She wasn't quite sure how it had happened or how she'd misunderstood and made this mistake.

It had been such a happy Wednesday afternoon. She had only felt a little guilt not mentioning where she was going and afterwards she knew that all would be revealed. He'd offered her a break, a career in advertising. She wasn't some young thing who could easily be deceived and manipulated. Yet thoughts of herself as a glamour model had turned her head, although she was middle aged with too much middle.

Somehow, she had fallen into this trap and the papers were proclaiming her guilt in bold print. What was she going to do? What legal recriminations might be awaiting her? She had no money and nothing of value to sell. Pay day loans were stupid and even crazier if you had no pay day. What would it mean if she had to go bankrupt? She had never intended to endanger her marriage, but how could she be forgiven after this?

She was only fifty-one, he was seventy-three, but admittedly looked like he was wearing well. Where-as she looked a good ten years older!

Surely they could throw the book at her for appearing in an ad for twenty percent discount on beds and bedding for over sixties.

Even worse - people would now think that was her real age!

THE SORRY TALE OF TED AND TALLULAH   *by Red Rose*

Finding a new doorway to spend the night in, Ted threw down his thick piece of cardboard, placing his dirty worn rucksack gently next to it. Sore, chilblained hands rolled out the old sleeping bag, his bones creaking as he lowered himself slowly down, pulling it over his legs; it had no zip, but he was grateful for what little warmth it provided him and Tallulah in the winter months.

Those cold winter days were bleak and the cold winter nights would be even bleaker were it not for Tallulah. He had stumbled upon her by chance, when he was rifling through the bins in an upmarket area of the town, hoping to find some out of date food that had been thrown away. He was transfixed when he caught a glimpse of her out of the corner of his eye. It was love at first sight as he stared down at the empty bottle of rum. There she was, a beautiful hula girl on the label, gazing right back. It may have been a trick of the light but he was sure she winked at him. Bending down he rescued her from the perils of the blue recycling box, stuffing her into his backpack along with a half-eaten loaf of bread. He named her there and then, without hesitation, Tallulah.

Ted was never lonely as she had been with him since then. They had been travelling together for nearly two years now, and every night when he lay her down, she watched over him as he slept. Sometimes on an evening when he'd had a particularly bad day he would talk to her, and in his head she would answer him. He didn't care she was a label on a bottle, she kept him going. It was the longest relationship he had ever had and he treasured and loved her.

That night started out the same as any other, he fished in his rucksack and placed Tallulah his hula girl tenderly next to him, and although it was particularly chilly he didn't feel the cold as he cradled her in his arms, gradually drifting off to sleep. He would never know how, but in the early hours of the morning his grip must have slackened and she'd rolled out of his arms, out of the doorway and onto the pavement.

The next morning Ted awoke to the loud noise of traffic on the road and felt next to him for Tallulah, but she was gone. With a sense of dread, he scrambled to his feet, moving on to the pavement as quickly as his old bones would allow.

"Nooooo... not my hula girl," he sobbed. He fell to his knees grief-stricken, as the sound of breaking glass filled the air, and the recycling truck trundled off into the distance.

Chapter Twelve

"Painting is poetry that is seen rather than felt, and poetry is painting that is felt rather than seen"

Leonardo da Vinci

Poetry

Our final chapter is a miscellaneous mix of wonderful poems by Guest Writer - Linda French (Fuchsia Rose).

POEMS *by Fuchsia Rose*

JANUARY SALES

High Street shopping never fails
To amuse me at the sales.
To place it in commercial jargon -
Everybody loves a 'bargain'.
Women's arms with bags they hang
Like a pert orangutan.
With the bargains in the store
The customers play tug-'o'-war,
How they vie tooth and nail
To get ahead and win the sale.
It leaves me feeling hot and flustered
But January makes them mustered,
To keep their New Year's resolutions
Of economical solutions.
And people never lose the will
To queue forever at the till,
So get your purse out - Do not quail,
Let's all rush down to the sale!

THE GOOSE AND THE GANDER

The feminine is goose,
The masculine is gander.
"What's good for the goose… "
Perhaps that is slander?
Time to turn around
This chauvinist abuse –
"What's good for the gander
Is good for the goose!"

THE UMBRELLA

Love's umbrella
Offers shelter
In life's stormy
Helter-skelter.
Whatever life sends
To defy us
True love will always
 Stand right by us.
The strength of love
Is truly endless
She'll stand by you
When you're friendless.
Love can bring
Both joy and woe
But love's a friend,
Never a foe.
And love is caring,
Love's to share,
Love is always
Waiting there.

WHAT IS LOVE?

Alone,
Like an island
In a sea of hate,
Love is the dictator,
That semi-religion absorbing
All faiths and denominations,
It's ambit as incalculable as pi.

And what is love?
Love is from the sublime
To the ridiculous,
Enduring the aeons of time
Through the thorns of reality.
The syndrome aches
In this celestial paradox
Of no-man's land
Like a vintage wine,
The anchor of life,
Maturing with age.

So what is love?
The open door to freedom,
Love's oasis is
An umbrella from the storm,
The eighth wonder of the world,
Superior warfare,
The answer.

You've come to the end of the book, but -

"Don't cry because it's over, smile because it happened"

Dr. Seuss

The End

Made in the USA
Lexington, KY
01 July 2018